Shandra Higheagle Mystery Books

Double Duplicity

Tarnished Remains

Deadly Aim

Murderous Secrets

Killer Descent

Reservation Revenge

Yuletide Slayings

Reservation Revenge

A Shandra Higheagle Mystery

Paty Jager

Windtree Press

RESERVATION REVENGE

Contact Information: info@windtreepress.com

Windtree Press
Hillsboro, Oregon
http://windtreepress.com

Cover Art by Christina Keerins

Published in the United States of America

ISBN 9781944973063

Special Thanks to:

Carmen Peone for helping me keep the reservation life factual.

Crimescene Yahoo group for being there to answer my medical and murder questions.

My son-in-law in law enforcement who keeps my cops real.

And my niece, Maggie Holcomb, who keeps my sentences straight and timing in order.

I couldn't write one of these mysteries without any of these resources.

Thank you all!

Chapter One

"Ella, what do you want?" Shandra Higheagle pleaded as she stood looking up into the clouds that formed her deceased grandmother's face. The droplets of rain falling on Shandra's face were warm and salty. Tears.

She bolted upright in bed. A dream. But Ella, Grandmother, had been crying sad tears. The worry lines on her grandmother's wrinkled face had been deeper, more defined. Shandra reached over to wake Ryan but found cold sheets.

She clicked on the light and remembered work had required him to stay at his house in Warner the last week. His job as a Weippe County Sheriff's Detective kept him there as much as he stayed with her. She rubbed her hand back and forth on the empty side of the bed. It had taken her more than a year to overcome her fear of letting anyone close, and now all she could think of was talking to Ryan. He understood her dreams better than she did.

She glanced at the clock on the bedside table. Three. Her hand hovered over her cell phone. Something was wrong, that was the only thing to explain her grandmother crying. But what? And was it worth waking Ryan when she didn't have any rational reason?

Sheba crawled up onto the bed. Shandra wrapped her arms around her huge, furry, multi-colored dog and hugged her. "I'll wait until morning to call Ryan."

The dog nudged her big muzzle into Shandra's chest, pushing her back against the pillows. "Okay, I can take a hint. Turn off the lights and let's get some sleep." She chuckled, turned out the light, and patted the dog taking up Ryan's half of the bed.

~*~

Shandra woke to strains of Ella Fitzgerald and Louis Armstrong's *Dream a Little Dream of Me* from her phone.

She glanced at the clock. Six.

Then the phone. Aunt Jo.

Her heart raced in her chest. Was a problem on the reservation the reason Ella was crying in her dream? Shandra sat up straight and stroked her finger across the small screen. "What's wrong?"

"Shandra, we need your help." Aunt Jo sounded close to tears.

"What's happened?" She shoved the hair off her face and stood, walking out of her room. She'd grown close to her aunt the last year and a half. When she hurt so did Shandra.

"The police were here along with an FBI agent. They think Coop killed Arthur Randal."

The distress in her aunt's voice made Shandra's stomach churn. "What does Coop say about this?"

"We don't know. We haven't seen him since Saturday night." A deep inhale and she added, "I know my boy. He wouldn't kill anyone."

Shandra didn't think Coop was a killer either. "Gather all the information you can. I'll be there in five hours."

"Thank you," Aunt Jo said and hung up.

Shandra continued to the kitchen. She started a pot of coffee and dialed Ryan.

"Morning beautiful," Ryan said, his voice still rough from sleep.

Any other time his familiar greeting would have made her smile. Right now there was too much on her mind. "Grandmother came to me in a dream last night. She was crying." Shandra didn't wait for Ryan to comment. "Aunt Jo called this morning. The tribal police and FBI are looking for Coop. They think he killed someone."

"I can check my sources and see what I can find out." His voice was all business.

She smiled. That was one of the things she loved about the man, he could switch from lover to policeman in a second. "That would be helpful. I told Aunt Jo I'd be there in five hours." Two steps took her to the fridge. She pulled out the milk and grabbed a bowl and cereal from the cupboard.

"I know you've managed to solve several murders, but I don't think you should get in the middle of a federal investigation." Concern and protectiveness echoed in his voice.

"My family needs me. I won't sit here when I can give my aunt support." She poured the cereal and milk into the bowl. Sheba nudged her. The dog's soulful brown eyes studied Shandra while her big fluffy tail swung back and forth with enough force to make Shandra's bare legs cold.

"I understand wanting to help your family. Just don't get in the way of the investigation. I can't help you if you get in trouble." Again, his concern touched her, but once she'd discovered her Nez Perce family wanted her in their lives, she'd made a vow to herself to be there for them, whatever they needed.

"I promise to stay clear of the FBI."

Sheba started talking and pacing.

"I have to go. Sheba needs fed and let out and I have to fill Lil in on what to do while I'm gone."

She pulled the phone from her ear and started to hit the off button when she heard Ryan.

"Shandra, be careful. I'll see if I can get some days off and join you."

Her heart thumped in her chest. She held the phone back to her ear. "That would be nice, but don't worry if you can't."

"You can't brush me off that easy," he joked.

"I know, you sheepherders are like ticks."

He laughed and hung up.

Her heart hummed with happiness. Who would have thought a girl raised on a cattle ranch would have fallen for the son of a sheep rancher? And one that understood her need to explore the heritage that was kept from her for so long.

"Come on, girl." She fed Sheba. After the dog cleaned up her bowl, Shandra let her outside. She stood at the back door and inhaled the summer scents of pine and wild rose. Her backyard butted up against the majestic pines of Huckleberry Mountain. This ranch was her sanctuary.

Returning to the kitchen, she ate her cereal and moved to the bedroom to dress and pack. Luckily, she was between projects right now. She and Lil had just sent out her latest vase to a gallery in the mid-west.

Dressed and her overnight bag stowed in her Jeep, she headed for the barn. Lil, her hired help, lived in the old tack room in the barn. The woman had come with the place like a stray cat. Having grown up on the ranch, she didn't know any other place. After her grandparents passed, she'd squatted on the land until the owners discovered her and kicked her off. Hearing the woman's story, Shandra had offered her a job and had never regretted it. Though she wished the eccentric woman would live in the apartment over the studio rather than the tack room in the barn.

She spotted the older woman in the far side of the corral. Her standard purple clothing made her stick out in the corral among the browns and whites of the horses. Today the eccentric woman sported a short-sleeved, button-front blouse covered in purple flowers.

Her jeans were purple as well as the rhinestone studded cap on her spiky white hair.

"Lil!" Shandra called, standing at the corral gate.

Lil pat the horse closest to her on the neck and strode across the corral.

Lewis, the orange cat that was usually draped around Lil's neck, rubbed against Shandra's legs. "Good morning, Lewis."

The cat meowed and continued his figure eight around her legs.

Sheba bounded up to the corral, her tongue lapping at the drool dangling from her lips.

"What are all of you doing up so early?" Lil asked, stepping through the gate.

"I received a call from my aunt. She needs me." Shandra knew her employee didn't mind hanging out on the mountain by herself, but it bothered her.

"Good thing you finished that vase last week." Her eyes narrowed. "You get more work done when that cop ain't hanging around here."

Shandra smiled. Lil was still combative about Ryan. Even after he'd saved both of them from harm more than once.

"I don't know how long I'll be gone, but I'll check in every day."

Lil nodded. "You always do."

"Have I told you lately how thankful I am that you are here?" She was. Without the feisty woman, she wouldn't be able to keep her horses and would have to find a place for Sheba when she did lectures and workshops. And the woman was a huge help in the art studio.

"Don't get all mushy. I don't want to live anywhere else, so you're stuck with me." Lil picked up Lewis, draping the large cat around her neck like a fur stole. "Want me to glaze those coasters?"

"Please." The coasters made from the clay found on her property and etched with the mountain's likeness helped pick up the slack between her art sales. The local businesses sold them as souvenirs in the shops of Huckleberry Resort.

The woman walked away, leaving Shandra to say good-bye to Sheba and head for the Colville Reservation four hours away.

Chapter Two

Shandra drove by the gas station and trading post at the Agency. The government community of the reservation. The parking lot had more vehicles and people than she'd witnessed on her previous visits to the reservation.

She continued through Nespelem and up the Nespelem river valley to her aunt and uncle's horse ranch. Her stomach clenched at the sight of a Tribal Police vehicle at the side of the road leading to the ranch.

At the ranch buildings, she recognized Velma's car. The woman was her aunt's cousin and of the Seven Drums religion like her grandmother had been. Shandra parked and stepped out of the Jeep.

Andy, Coop's younger brother, strode toward her from the barn. His lips were pressed closed in a grim line, but his eyes questioned her. He knew something.

Before she could ask questions, Aunt Jo opened the back door to the house and motioned for her to hurry.

Stopping long enough to make full eye contact with Andy, she said, "You know where he is."

He nodded.

She searched the hills and terrain that encompassed the ranch. "Up there?" Her chin came up slightly as she tipped her head toward the hills.

Again, he nodded.

"Do your parents know?"

He shook his head.

"Saddle up two horses. After I visit with your mom, we're going to go talk to him."

Andy's eyes brightened and he smiled. "I was hoping you'd say that."

Bouncing around the fact she knew where Coop was and his parents didn't, she walked to the house. She should tell them what Andy told her, but at the same time, she wondered at Coop's hiding. If he hadn't killed someone, which she believed, he didn't have a reason to hide.

"What were you and Andy talking about?" Aunt Jo asked.

"He's worried about Coop." She didn't like lying to her aunt, but she needed more information, and Coop's side of things before she decided the best plan of action. It was obvious the police were looking for him from the officer sitting at the end of the driveway.

Velma handed her a cup of tea after she'd sat down at the kitchen table. They locked gazes and she saw grandmother had been in her cousin's dreams as well.

Shandra turned her attention to her aunt. "Tell me who Coop supposedly killed and why."

Aunt Jo sat down beside her. The woman's long slender fingers grasped Shandra's wrist as if she needed the contact to anchor her. "The police arrived here late last night. I'd just started getting worried about Coop. I knew he'd went to a party at Buffalo Lake on Saturday night and figured he'd spent the night at a friend's house afterwards. But when he didn't arrive for dinner last night…" She swiped at a tear slipping out of her eye. "He never misses Sunday dinner if he's not away at school."

She placed a hand over her aunt's. "When the police arrived?"

"I thought they were going to tell me that he was in an accident. Not—not that he was wanted for killing someone." Aunt Jo's bottom lip trembled and her head quivered as if refusing everything.

Her uncle strode into the room. "Shandra." He nodded to her and knelt beside his wife. "Jo, everything will be all right."

The distraught woman stared at her husband.

He reached out, touching her cheek. "We have good boys. They are wrong to think Coop would hurt anyone."

"Who did he supposedly kill?" Shandra asked, thinking she might learn more from Andy as they rode out to see Coop.

"Arthur Randal." Uncle Martin stood and walked to the stove.

She glanced at Velma. The woman nodded toward the living room.

"I'll be right back," Shandra said to her aunt and pried the woman's fingers from her wrist. "I promise. It was a long drive. I need…"

Jo's face reddened. "I'm so sorry. I—"

"You were worried. I'll be right back." She walked out of the kitchen and felt Velma on her heels. She stopped at the bathroom door. "Are you following me in?" she asked, grinning at the astounded look on the other woman's face.

"No. But it would be easier to talk without being overheard. Ays." The twinkle in the larger woman's eyes made Shandra laugh.

"I'll be quick."

Exiting the bathroom, she found Velma hovering in the hallway.

"Did Aunt Minnie come to you?" she asked in a whisper.

"Yes. Last night. She was crying, that's all." A chill chased across Shandra's skin remembering the dream.

"This is bad. Arthur Randal's family has had it out for the Higheagles for years. Your great-grandfather had a magnificent horse. His offspring won many races, on the reservation and off. But your great-grandfather refused to allow anyone to use him as a stallion. He was only to breed Higheagle horses. Arthur's great-grandfather released several of his mares into a Higheagle pasture. Before your great-grandfather discovered them, the stallion had covered every one.

17

Since then the Randals and Higheagles have not talked to one another. The children are not allowed to play together."

Shandra couldn't believe there was still such a feud going on. "Then how did Arthur and Coop end up at the same place?"

"There was a big party at Buffalo Lake. Feuds and fights are forgotten when alcohol is available." Velma's face scrunched in disgust.

"Did the two young men know about the feud?"

"Everyone on the reservation knows of the feud. It has been spoken of for many years and kept alive." Velma heaved her wide chest out like she was proud of carrying on the feud.

"But would the boys fight over a decades' old feud after drinking too much?" She'd witnessed drunk young men at college and seldom did they have enough brains functioning to think about anything other than what was happening at that moment.

"It was Sandy."

Shandra locked gazes with Velma. "Sandy, the girl Coop is head over heels about?"

"The same."

That could make this a crime of passion. She remembered her trip to Omak with Coop and how he'd talked about Sandy non-stop. "What happened?"

"Arthur attacked Sandy, and Coop knocked him around." Velma started back down the hall. "But according to Andy, Arthur was alive and back drinking when Coop went looking for Sandy."

Back in the kitchen, Jo was busy at the stove and

Martin was sitting at the table, a cup of coffee clutched between his hands.

"Velma filled me in," she said, walking up to Jo. "It sounds like Andy knows the most about this. He and I can go for a ride where he feels more comfortable talking about it."

Jo nodded, but she saw Martin perk up. He stood. "I'll walk you out to the barn."

On her way by the Jeep, Shandra reached in and grabbed her ball cap. The sun in this area was brutal all summer long. She slipped her braid through the opening in the back and pulled the front down, blocking the bright rays of sunlight.

"Andy knows where Coop is, doesn't he?" Martin strode beside her.

"I'm not saying yes or no. Best if not everyone in the family is helping him." Shandra stopped halfway between the house and barn. "I know Aunt Jo called because she thinks I can help find the real killer. I won't have Ryan's help on the reservation. I can't promise you anything other than I'll try to find the truth." She glanced up at the fluffy white cloud hanging over the ranch. "Grandmother is sad that this is happening. I think she'll help me."

Martin nodded and walked back to the house.

Shandra walked over to where Andy stood with two saddled appaloosa horses.

Chapter Three

Shandra had noticed the bulging saddlebags tied to the back of Andy's saddle as soon as she took to the trail behind him. An hour later, they'd traveled over two hills and were now trailing a trickle of water flowing down a small ravine.

"How did he get here?" she asked, batting at the dust kicked up by Andy's horse.

"I smuggled him in after we heard the cops were looking for him." Andy slowed his horse, so they could ride side by side. "He didn't kill Arthur. He was with Sandy, then his friend Lyle, until I picked him up and brought him here."

"So he did catch up to her." She'd been wondering if the two had met after the altercation.

"Yeah. She was walking back and he picked her up." Andy dropped his gaze.

"What happened when he picked her up?"

"He was pissed. Sandy had blood on her face from where Arthur slapped her." Andy's face turned a deep crimson. "And her blouse was ripped. Her—" He motioned toward his chest. "Her boobs were showing some."

"You were with them?" He was the best eyewitness for Coop's defense.

"Yeah. I didn't want to stay at the lake after Coop beat up Arthur, so I ran after Coop and hopped in the back of his pickup." Andy grinned. "I figured he was going after Sandy and wouldn't want me along."

Shandra smiled. "You are your brother's best chance at proving he didn't kill Arthur."

His grin turned down. "That's the thing. When he discovered I was in the back of the pickup, he made me get out." He shrugged. "I caught a ride with the next person headed to town."

"So you don't know that Coop didn't go back to the lake." She thought about this. "What was his reaction to Sandy's ripped clothing?"

"I told you, pissed. He was talking about going back and making it so Arthur couldn't play basketball again." He stopped his horse and spun in the saddle to face her. "He didn't say kill him, he said hurt him so he couldn't play ball."

She agreed. That sounded more like the Coop she knew. He wouldn't take a life, but he knew what the other man lived for—sports.

Andy stopped and dismounted. "We're walking from here." He untied the saddlebags and headed up the side of the rocky ravine.

Shandra dismounted and followed, hoping there weren't any rattlesnakes in their path.

They climbed for about fifteen minutes before she spotted a small camouflage tent tucked under a pine tree. A camp stove, bucket, and lantern all sat beside the one-man tent.

Andy ducked his head into the tent. He stepped back and scanned the hillside. "He's not here. I guess we wait if you want to talk to him." He sat on a rock. She found a downed tree in the shade of the pine.

"Where could he have gone?" she asked, wondering how a young man studying to be part of the computer technology world felt being unplugged.

"He's either hiking or looking for food." Andy didn't seem the least bit worried about his brother.

"Does he have a gun?" She wasn't sure that would be a good thing. He was wanted for murder. Being found with a gun would make him look hostile.

"No. He's using a snare. Grandma Minnie taught us how to survive in the wild." Andy glanced up at the sun. "We've spent a week or two in these hills every summer seeing how well we could survive."

"I wish I had spent more time with Ella." Saying it out loud made her realize how much she really did wish she had been able to stay connected with her father's people. All those years she'd ignored it because her mother and step-father—the murderer of her father— had insisted she not let anyone know she was half Nez Perce.

"Why didn't you come see us sooner?" Andy asked. His round youthful face, which was usually so animated, had pulled a veil of no emotion across.

She'd witnessed this trait in all the youth she'd met at the reservation. It was an innate ability they had to keep anyone from seeing what they really thought or felt.

"My mother and step-father forbid me to tell anyone I was Nez Perce. They said it was for my own good. That people would treat me poorly if they knew." She sighed. "When I was small I thought they knew best. As I became older, it was just easier to forget that side of me and focus on my schooingl and getting out of Montana."

"You could have come here." He looked down at this fingers, buckling and unbuckling the strap on the saddle bag. "We wouldn't have made you try to be what you aren't."

Her lips quivered into a smile. "I know that now. If Grandmother hadn't summoned me to her funeral, I would still be wondering if I should show my face here or leave it be."

"My ella, was smart. She healed many with her herbs and her dreams." Andy stood. "He's coming."

Shandra stood and spun around. She didn't see anyone coming from any direction. "How do you know?"

"The quail were running, instead of walking, like something spooked them."

Before she could find the quail, Coop appeared. He wasn't his usual happy self. His long legs strode forcefully toward them. He stopped in front of her.

"I didn't kill Arthur," he said with such force, she

took a step back.

"I know you didn't. But hiding out here in the woods makes you look guilty." She sat back down on the log.

Coop crossed his legs and sat on the ground in front of her. Andy handed them each a bottle of water.

"Tell me what happened and why you think you should hide." She unscrewed the top of the bottle and took a drink.

Her tall cousin slumped forward, his forearms propped on his legs. He stared at the bottle in his hand. He told her basically the same things Andy had told her up to the point of him kicking Andy out of his pickup.

"What did you do after you kicked Andy out?" She stared at the top of his dark head.

"Sandy didn't want to go home looking like she did." He raised his head. "That bastard ripped her shirt when she refused..." His grip on the bottle popped the top off and water sloshed over his hand and legs.

"Where did you go?" She tried to ignore the anger. This young man was more volatile than she'd remembered him being.

"I took her to her cousin's. I knocked on the door and asked for Ruby. She followed me to the pickup, and Sandy broke into tears. Ruby said she'd take care of her. They disappeared around the back of the house." He shoved a hand through his hair.

"What did you do then?" This was crucial. He needed an alibi for the time of the killing.

"I drove back to see if Andy found a ride."

"All the way to the lake?" Fear for her cousin

squeezed her chest. *Please say you didn't go all the way back.*

"I met Lyle coming out and asked him if Andy was there. He said there wasn't anyone left, to come to his house. I spent the night there after trying to check on Sandy one more time." He took a long drink of water.

"How did you hear about Arthur's death?" She didn't like that there was a span of time no one could vouch for him.

"The next morning. Lyle's uncle came for coffee and was telling everyone that a fisherman found Arthur's body on the dock not far from where we partied. He didn't look at me. I asked him what else he knew. He said, the police were looking for me because one of Arthur's friends said he saw me walking around the point with Arthur." He crunched the water bottle. "I didn't go anywhere with Arthur. But if they have a witness, no one will believe me."

"That's why you're hiding? Because you don't think anyone will believe you weren't the last person to see Arthur?" Her stomach knotted with dread. An eyewitness was why the law wanted her cousin.

"Yes." He raised his face to take a drink, and she witnessed tears in his eyes.

She turned her attention to Andy. "Do you know who the witness is?"

"Not confirmed, but word is Dorsey."

Coop shot to his feet. "Dorsey? That's Arthur's best friend. He'd do anything to pin this on me. Both Arthur and Dorsey have had a grudge since the winter basketball tournament."

"Why?" She didn't understand a grudge over basketball. She also didn't understand a hundred year feud.

Andy waved Coop to sit. "The Higheagle team, me, Coop, and four cousins, shut the Randal team down during the tournament. Arthur's team had beat everyone in the bracket by intimidation and plain meanness. We came up against them for winner of our bracket." He smiled. "After the Randals sent two players to the hospital in other games, Mom made sure we had Oscar Whitfield for the ref. He isn't related to either family and he believes in clean games. We won because they fouled so much. Coop made thirty points on free throws."

She glanced at Coop. "You think this young man gave the police your name because you beat them with free throws?" It seemed like a lame reason to her for someone to be blamed for murder.

"There are boasting rights for some time when you win your bracket in the tournament. And to have a family that you are feuding with beat you…" Coop raised his hands and shrugged.

Shaking her head, she stood. "I don't understand that, but I do plan to have a talk with Dorsey and that nice police man sitting at the end of your lane."

Coop stood. "They know I'm here?"

"I think he's sitting there hoping you try to go home." She put a hand on his arm. "Are you going to be okay here by yourself?" The next words she knew he didn't want to hear. "You should turn yourself in. It's better to turn yourself in and tell your story than hide and look guilty."

He shook his head. "You don't understand. If Arthur's family thinks I'm guilty, they will make my life worse than hell."

"If you turn yourself in you don't look guilty. And we'll get a good public defender. One who will dig to find the truth."

"Not around here. Around here they rarely prosecute for the minor things. But this… I'm not safe anywhere with the Randals thinking I killed Arthur."

She didn't like the conviction in his voice. "I'll make sure you're kept safe. In jail and out. We'll find out who really killed Arthur."

"How? There's no way I'm giving myself up unless I know I have a good lawyer and I'll be safe in jail." Coop sat down, crossed his arms, and stared up at her with defiance.

Shandra mounted the horse and followed Andy back down to the ranch. It didn't make sense that Coop would rather hide from the police than stand up for himself and say he wasn't guilty.

"Is Coop right? The Randals will get to him even if he's in jail?" She watched Andy as he thought through her question.

"Yes. The law here doesn't always carry out justice. That is why Oliver is being so loud about getting the person who killed his grandson."

"I guess the first place I'm going is to see a lawyer." She didn't have a clue where to find one on the reservation, but she was pretty sure her aunt would know.

Chapter Four

"We have a cousin who is in the tribal law offices." Aunt Jo set two cups of tea on the kitchen table.

Shandra sat and gathered a cup into her hands even though the house was almost as hot as it was outside. "We do? Has anyone contacted the cousin to represent Coop?"

Her aunt shook her head. "I've been so worried about him not being found, I hadn't thought about him needing a lawyer."

She placed her hand over her aunt's. "I can tell you he's fine."

The older woman stared into her eyes. "You saw him or mother told you?"

A smiled crept onto Shandra's lips. For her staying away from her family for so long, it didn't take long for her aunt to believe in her and her dreams. "I can't tell you. That way if you are asked you know nothing about where Coop could be and haven't heard from him."

Her aunt's eyes widened and worry flashed in their dark depths. "If anyone finds out you know something, you aren't safe."

"Why wouldn't I be safe? I haven't done anything."

"The Randals will want revenge for the death of Arthur. If they think you are helping Coop, you could be hurt."

Shandra shook off any concerns about the dead man's family. There was no reason to come after her, she was looking for the real killer. "How do I contact my cousin, the lawyer?"

"Liz Piney works at the government center. She's an assistant public defender." Aunt Jo put a hand on her arm. "Are you going to talk to her?"

"Yes. I'll get Coop representation. Then he can turn himself in knowing he won't be railroaded, and we can focus on finding out who really killed Arthur." Shandra picked up her purse and headed out the door.

"Only talk to Liz. No one else. The Randals have family in the courts as well," Aunt Jo called from the back steps.

Shandra raised her hand, acknowledging she'd heard her aunt and climbed into her Jeep. She didn't know what to expect, but hoped her cousin, the Assistant Public Defender could help Coop.

~*~

Shandra pulled into the circular drive of the newly built Colville Confederated Tribes Headquarters and parked in the west side lot. According to Aunt Jo, the old agency building had burned down a few years prior. After much debate and pencil scratching, the current building was designed and constructed. The beautiful, three-story, concrete building painted orange and rust was a contemporary piece of architecture on the cusp of old, faded one and two-story buildings that housed the other agency businesses that either didn't want or hadn't been able to move into the new structure.

Doors swished open when she approached the entrance. Inside, the sunlight shone through large windows, highlighting the curved blue, tan, and brown tiles on the floor representing the Columbia River, a natural resource that had provided sustenance to the tribes of the Reservation for hundreds of years.

Not seeing any signs, she walked up to the woman standing behind what resembled a registration desk in a hotel.

"May I help you?" a woman younger than Shandra asked.

"Yes. I'm looking for the public defender's office, specifically Liz Piney."

"You'll find those offices on the second floor in the west wing."

"Thank you." Shandra turned away then turned back. "And how do I get to the second floor?"

"Stairway to your left."

She nodded her thanks and walked down the hall to a wide stairway leading to the second floor. At the top of the stairs she encounter blank doors and an area that appeared to be for waiting. Walking into the waiting area, she wondered if she should have called and made an appointment.

"May I help you?" asked a young woman, sitting behind a desk.

"I would like to speak to Ms. Liz Piney."

The young woman gave her a look as if she'd just asked to see a high profile actor.

"Do you have an appointment?" She ran a pencil down a date book to her left.

"No. I would like to talk to her about my cousin. He's in trouble and I thought she could give me some advice." Shandra drew her lips into a friendly smile.

"Who are you and who is the cousin?" The woman poised the pencil over a square note pad.

Due to the interest of the three people occupying the chairs in the small lobby, Shandra leaned forward and said softly, "Could you tell her Shandra Higheagle is here to see her."

The young woman's eyes widened and her mouth formed an O before she shut her lips and picked up the phone. The same pencil she'd run down the date book and hovered over the note pad, now tapped three numbers on the desk phone.

"Ms. Piney, there's a Shandra Higheagle here to see you." She listened. "Yes." The phone settled on the cradle and the receptionist stood. "Follow me, please."

Shandra smiled and followed the receptionist down the hall and into what appeared to be a small conference room.

"Ms. Piney will be with you shortly. Can I get you coffee, tea, or water?"

"Tea would be nice." Setting her fringed purse on the table, she took a seat facing the door. She hadn't taken the time to learn anything about her cousin.

The young woman returned with a steaming mug of water, a tea bag, spoon, and saucer.

"Thank you." Shandra picked up the tea bag.

"Ms. Piney will be right in when she finishes with a client." The woman strode out of the room, closing the door behind her.

Shandra studied the art on the walls and pulled out her phone. She text Ryan she'd made it to her aunt's and was waiting to speak with a public defender.

How is your cousin? He text back.

Worried. They have a witness who puts him with the dead man, but Coop insists he was never alone with the man. She sipped her tea, waiting for his response.

Sounds like he has good reason. Let the investigator working for the Public Defender find the truth.

She couldn't in good conscience agree. If Grandmother came to her in a dream, she had to follow the clue and an investigator would think she was crazy if she suggested he follow her dream.

Shandra, let the professionals on the reservation do the investigating.

Please.

She smiled. Ryan had learned ordering her around only made her dig her heels in more. *I'll try. But if Grandmother shows me clues, you know I have to follow them.*

The door knob jiggled.

Gotta go. She shoved her phone into her purse as a woman her height and just as slender, entered the room. Her dark hair was pulled back tight. A pencil stuck out of the wide, braided bun at the back of her head. She wore a bright-colored, tailored shirt and brown slacks. A pretty coral polish on her toes drew attention to her feet and beaded sandals.

"Shandra." She held out a long-fingered hand with trimmed fingernails. "I'm Liz Piney, your cousin."

"Pleased to meet you." Shandra extended her hand.

They shook hands, and Liz took the seat next to where Shandra had sat. "Are you here about Coop Elwood?"

She liked that the woman got straight to the heart of things. So unlike the elders she'd met who took their time coming to the topic they really wished to talk about.

"Yes. He believes—"

"You've talked to him?" She leaned closer and held out a hand. "Give me a dollar."

"I don't understand?" Shandra stared down at the palm her cousin set in front of her.

"I need you to pay me to represent you if you've been talking to a fugitive. That way I'm not legally bound to tell the courts what you tell me." She wiggled her fingers.

Shandra dug into her purse and found a five dollar bill. She placed it in the woman's hand.

"Good. Sorry, but if you had told me anything without being my client, I would have had to let the courts know. Now, I take it you've seen Coop?"

"Yes. He heard there's an eyewitness, which is why he's hiding. He says he was never alone with the dead man and whoever claims that is lying. He doesn't trust the courts, or the Randals, will find him innocent with a witness." Shandra pulled out another five dollar bill. "We, the family, would like you to represent Coop. If he knows he has a good lawyer, he'll turn himself in."

"Hold onto your money. He's an accused man. I don't have to take a retainer for him. Tell him I will represent him as long as he swears he didn't kill Arthur Randal." She jotted down a number on the back of a business card. "Talk to him. Have him call me, and we'll meet at the police station when he turns himself in."

"Another thing. He said the Randals may try to harm him even in jail. Is that true?"

Her cousin leaned back in her chair and sighed. "Unfortunately, the police around here can't keep up with every threat that is thrown between families. But knowing Oliver Randal, I'll make sure Coop isn't allowed any visitors other than family."

For the first time since the dream, Shandra had hope. "Thank you." She took the card. "I'll get this and a phone to him."

Liz stood and peered down at her. "I've heard about the murders you've solved. There is still talk of how you discovered your father's death wasn't an accident." Liz bent her head a moment then continued. "Those murders were off the reservation. And you had the help of your boyfriend, a cop. Don't try to investigate here. You don't know the relatives of Arthur Randal. If you say the wrong thing to one of them, you could find yourself in trouble. I have an investigator and the FBI is in on this. We'll discover the truth without your help."

She nodded, but had her ankles crossed under the table. She couldn't agree to anything, knowing Ella would come to her and provide the clues they needed to keep Coop free.

Chapter Five

Shandra left the Colville Tribal Headquarters feeling hopeful. Liz appeared competent. She had an investigator, and the FBI would be looking for the truth as well. Though considering her last experience with the FBI, she wasn't sure she trusted her cousin's life to a federal agent.

She sat at the stop sign to the highway and glanced down the road. Her last visit here she'd stopped at the Community Center to meet her aunt. Today, there were four times as many vehicles at the center. She didn't think Aunt Jo would go to work, worrying about Coop. But on the off chance she had, it wouldn't hurt to give her the news Liz would represent her son.

Accelerating her Jeep across the highway, she eased into the packed parking lot. A man with long gray braids stood on the steps of the building. She stepped out of her Jeep and worked her way through the men, women, teenagers, and children gathered in the parking lot.

"We will split up into groups of threes and search this reservation for Arthur's killer!" shouted the man on the steps.

Fear slithered up her spine and lodged in her throat. These people were looking for Coop. The angry faces and cheers of agreement lodged a ball of dread in her chest. If one of these people found him, she had a pretty good idea he wouldn't make it to jail unharmed.

A man in dress slacks and a white shirt rolled up to his elbows, stepped up beside the older man. He raised his hands. Sunlight highlighted his blonde hair and glinted off his sunglasses. A middle-aged man in a police uniform stood to the man's left.

The well-dressed man nodded to the group. "We want Coop Elwood brought in peacefully. Don't bring your longstanding feud into this federal matter."

He had to be the FBI agent. And the man standing beside him had to be part of the reservation police force. She needed to talk to both of them and see what she could learn.

"We don't want you launching a search party and causing more trouble by trespassing. Keep your eyes and ears open and tell me if you hear anything about Elwood's whereabouts. Now go home and listen." He waved his hands as if shooing away an unwanted flock of birds.

"Do as Agent Weatherly asks. From what we have learned so far this was not related to the feud. Go home." The police officer next to the agent turned to the older man with gray braids. "Tell them to go home, Oliver. They are your family."

"We'll go home for now, but we will find him." The older man stared at the police officer.

Shandra had managed to shove herself to the front of the crowd. She watched the battle of wills between the three men on the steps.

"Oliver. I don't want to arrest you, but I will if you try to hinder this investigation." The police officer took a step toward Oliver Randal.

He narrowed his eyes. His arms crossed over his chest.

"Father. Come. This won't bring Arthur back." A short, stout woman dressed in blue shorts and a large, baggy T-shirt walked up the steps and grabbed the older man by the arm.

"We won't be disgraced by another Higheagle." He pulled his arm away from the woman.

"You cannot continue to hold a grudge for actions that did not happen to you." She once again took hold of his arm. "Come now." She tugged and this time he walked down the steps.

At the bottom, not ten feet from Shandra, he shouted, "We will not rest!"

The crowd roared to life and followed the man and his daughter like a swarm of wasps after a meal.

Shandra strode to the steps while the FBI agent and the police officer were still in conversation.

"Excuse me." She traversed the steps and stood at the top.

"You're excused," said the FBI agent, Weatherly.

He lifted his sunglasses, and she peered into green eyes.

She held out her hand. "I'm Shandra Higheagle."

He grasped her hand and held it. "Agent Frank Weatherly."

Dragging her fingers from his grip, she extended her hand to the police officer. "And you are?"

"Tribal Police Chief Samuel George." He barely touched her hand. "Why are you here?"

The accusatory tone had her biting back a retort. Instead, she smiled. "I'm here to tell you, Coop is willing to turn himself in now that he has legal representation."

Both men stared at her as if she'd just dangled a twenty ounce steak in front of them.

"You know where he is?" Chief George asked.

"Take us to him," Agent Weatherly said.

She held up her hands. "I just retained his lawyer. I still have to relay the information to him." She narrowed her eyes. "He didn't kill anyone. Once he turns himself in, I don't want you stopping the investigation."

Chief George grinned. "We have an eyewitness that says your cousin was with Arthur before he died."

She shook her head. "You'll need to check out Coop's actions. He wasn't near Arthur when he was killed."

Agent Weatherly stepped between her and the chief. "You go tell Coop to turn himself in, and we'll do the investigating. If he gives us his account, and we can verify he wasn't near the lake at the time the coroner estimates the time of death, we'll look elsewhere."

She didn't like his condescending smile or the chief nodding behind the agent.

It was clear neither man would try to find the real killer. They both felt they had all the evidence they needed.

Without muttering another word, because it would be pointless, she pivoted, walked down the steps, and strode to her Jeep. The parking lot held only half a dozen vehicles since the Randal family left. She didn't see Aunt Jo's pickup. With the rowdy group she'd come upon, it was a good thing Jo stayed home.

A quick glance in her rearview mirror revealed the FBI agent talking on his phone and watching the sky. Great. All she needed was someone in the air watching as she contacted Coop.

~*~

Shandra headed straight for her aunt's ranch. Driving slowly, she noticed a helicopter hovering over the hills. The agent had called out a helicopter to follow her. It didn't make sense. She told them Coop was willing to turn himself in. And that's what she'd help him do. There was no way she'd let the feds, or anyone else, arrest her cousin when he was willing to come in peacefully.

She waved to the officer still sitting at the end of the drive.

He waved back.

She shook her head at the strange events. He watched the road, yet waved as if she were a neighbor passing by as she continued to the house. She spotted

Andy working with a horse in the corrals. After parking, she walked over. The faint sound of the helicopter thudded in the background. She placed her arms over the top rail of the corral and watched her young cousin put the horse through a range of movements without touching the animal.

He started around the corral, keeping the horse moving ahead of him when he spotted her.

"Whoa," he said to the horse who stopped and stood, watching him.

Andy walked over to the corral. "Did you get Liz to represent Coop?"

"Yes. She wants him to call her and she'll meet him at the police station." She glanced up. "I also met the FBI agent who has a helicopter following me."

Andy didn't look up. "They've been flying over the ranch all day."

"We'll have to wait until tonight to get Coop. Hopefully we can sneak out without them finding us." She didn't like having to wait that long to get him to the safety of the jail after seeing the vengeance in the Randal family.

Andy pulled out his cell phone. "A cousin has him tucked in at their barn. I called him after we talked to Coop and told him to get him closer to town." He punched in several numbers. "Hey, how'd the hunting go?" He listened. "Good. Can you take some meat to town?"

Shandra smiled at the coded message. She doubted anyone had bugged Andy's or any of the family's phones.

He held his hand out. "What's the number?"

She dug Liz's business card out of her pocket, holding it up for him to read.

Andy read the number. "You write that down? Ok. Have him call." He shoved the phone in his pocket. "All's good."

"I hope so. The Randals were talking of getting up a search party to try and find Coop."

He shook his head. "That's not good. He should be safe soon. Then we have to find who really killed Arthur."

Chapter Six

Shandra sat in the guest room, which was Coop's bedroom. Dinner with Aunt Jo, Uncle Martin, and Andy had been quiet. Everyone wondering if Coop made it to the jail and Liz met him. She had a note pad on her lap, making a list of the people she would talk to tomorrow.

The house phone rang.

She glanced down at her phone sitting on the bed beside her. She'd checked in with Lil but didn't want to call Ryan, knowing he'd repeat his concerns for her trying to find out who killed Arthur.

Someone ran up the stairs. Andy burst through the door. "That was Liz. She said Coop is safe in the jail. She's talked to him and is sending her investigator out to talk to the people who were at the party. She wants me to make a list of the people I remember."

"I'm glad she's getting started so quickly and Coop

is safe." She patted the bed next to her.

He crossed the room and sat. She showed him the list she was making. "Can you think of anyone else I might need to talk to?"

His face reddened. "I know Coop likes Sandy more than any other girl. But she does go out with a couple other guys when Coop is at school."

She didn't like the idea some girl was playing with Coop's affections. However, that there could be other lovelorn men out to avenge Sandy was helpful to Coop. "Who are they?" She poised her pen over the sheet with the other names.

"Billy Crow, Dorsey—"

"Really? The same person who says he saw Coop with Arthur." That was very interesting. Could be Dorsey was covering for his own crime. She put a star by his name on the list.

Andy nodded. "Steve Wood."

"That makes three men besides Coop who could have avenged Sandy." She glanced up from the notepad. "How many of them were at the lake that night?"

"Dorsey, Billy Crow, and I think Steve. Anyway, I saw his jacked-up truck there."

That gave her more suspects. What worried her was her gentle cousin getting his heart broken. "Does Coop know Sandy has this many men interested in her?"

"He's been away to school and only seeing her when he's home on long weekends. I don't think he knows she's been seeing anyone but him." He shrugged. "I didn't want to be the one to tell him. I was hoping she'd say something or he'd see how she acted around the others."

She tapped the pen against her bottom lip, staring at Andy. "This is interesting. Before this is over, we'll have to find a way to show Coop that Sandy may not be for him. He deserves a girl who only has eyes for him."

Andy grinned. "Yeah. Like Mom and Dad. Or you and Ryan."

Shandra stared at her cousin. "What do you mean, me and Ryan? You've only met him once, and we aren't talking anything long term."

"You both have the look." He nodded.

"The look?"

"Yeah. When you look at each other anyone else can see you are talking with your eyes." He stood. "If you want someone to go with you when you talk to people I could go."

She knew no one would be open with her. That's why she'd already asked Velma to go with her to talk to the people on her list. "I'm good. Velma is going with me."

"Good choice. If you can't charm it out of them, she can scare it out. Ays!" He laughed and left the room.

Shandra shook her head and laughed. What he said was true. It appeared many members of the community feared Velma. She wasn't sure if it was because of her size, her loud voice, her dominate personality, or her affiliation with the Seven Drums Religion.

A text jingled on her phone. She glanced at the

screen. Ryan.

Did your cousin turn himself in?

Yes. And another cousin is his public defender. She shoved the list into her purse. He couldn't see it but she'd feel less guilty not staring at it.

Is it wise to have a family member represent him?

In this case, yes. That way we know he'll get the best representation. Too many people have connections to the family of the murdered man. There was a large group at the community center today planning to find Coop and do him harm. She shuddered thinking of the lynch mob mentality she'd witnessed today.

Her phone played the jazz tune she used for her ring. Ryan.

"You didn't have to call." She tried to sound cheerful, but she knew he was only going to talk about her keeping safe.

"What were you doing at the community center? You need to stay at the ranch and comfort your aunt, not get into trouble where I can't help you." His tone was stern, but she heard the undertone of worry. She couldn't be mad at him for his concern.

"Nothing will happen to me. Liz, the public defender, is putting her investigator on the case." She didn't plan to tell him about the list of suspects.

"Let them do their jobs. There isn't any reason for you to try and solve this. It sounds like your cousin knows what she's doing." His voice softened. "It's ironic, I could go to your ranch now, but you aren't there."

"If we—I mean Liz and the investigator, don't find

any good leads on the real killer in a couple of days, I'll come home. There's no sense my hanging around here when I can be working."

"I agree. Sometimes these things can take weeks or months."

She hoped it didn't take that long. Aunt Jo would be a wreck in a month, let alone longer than that.

"Do the reservation police seem competent?" he asked.

"I've only met the chief. He was a bit standoffish, but that could be because the FBI agent was standing next to him." She'd felt an aura of hostility from the chief. Agent Weatherly had come off too cocky for her liking.

"FBI agent? How did you meet those two?" Wariness was back in his voice.

"They were at the community center, tossing reason into the mob." There was no need to tell him her concerns about the agent. With luck she wouldn't run into him again.

"Did they calm the mob down?"

"Somewhat. They left and weren't as angry." She was going to steer clear of groups of people while she was on the reservation. She didn't know who could be a Randal and who wasn't.

"Good. Then it sounds like the police chief is respected."

She had to agree there. "Yes. It seemed so."

"I put out a request to a friend in the FBI to get a copy of the forensic report on the victim. He was curious about why I'd be interested in a case in another state and on a reservation."

"What did you tell him?" She knew Ryan would never lie, but what would be his excuse for wanting the information.

"I told him one of my future in-laws was a suspect in the death."

She sucked in air. They hadn't talked about marriage. She liked things the way they were, but she did once in a while envision Ryan in her future. Catching her breath, she asked, "And what did he say to that?"

"Congratulations." The exuberance in his voice made her smile and cringe.

"We haven't made any commitments to each other, especially not that big of one." Her heart thudded in her chest. She felt trapped and happy Ryan wanted to spend the rest of his life with her.

"I know we haven't talked about it, but I've been thinking about it."

Andy's comment came to her. She and Ryan did communicate without talking, but marriage?

"Shandra? Are you still there?" Panic infused his question.

"Yes. I'm here. I'm just…"

"Tell me you haven't thought about a future with me."

"I have, but now is a poor time to talk about this. There's so much on my mind." It was a lame excuse, but better than telling him marriage with anyone frightened her.

"You're right. This is something we should talk

about face to face. I'll check back in tomorrow. Stay safe." He hung up.

She stared at the phone and wondered what he was thinking. Did he take my excuse at face value or as a brush-off?

~*~

A young woman danced, spinning in the middle of a circle of young men. One she recognized as Coop. The others were faceless, but it was the young man lurking outside the circle that caught her attention. He also had no face, but he wasn't watching the girl, he watched one of the men. One of the faceless men fell, the girl screamed, and the young man outside the circle vanished.

Shandra sat up. The golden glow of morning light sifted in under the half-drawn shade. The early morning greeting of a rooster warbled through the open window. That was the sound that had pulled her from the dream.

She grabbed her phone and text Velma the names of the young men she wanted to see this morning. Through the whispers on the wind, her cousin would discover where each one could be found this morning, she had no doubt about Velma's talents.

Chapter Seven

Velma insisted on driving her 1985 Lincoln Town car. It was an automobile built for a tall, wide-bodied person.

Shandra slid into the passenger side. "Who are we talking to first?"

"Steve. He works at the Trading Post with Sandy." Velma backed out of her drive and floated the large car down the street.

"Will Sandy be there today?" She didn't think it would be a good idea to talk to the man about the woman if she was within sight.

"She took a week's vacation. She's pretty shook up." The woman glanced over at her. "Sources say she won't talk to anyone."

"I guess that means I'll have to be sympathetic and convincing as a friend when I see her this afternoon." Shandra wasn't going to reveal to her cousin that she knew how Sandy felt. After several years of living with an abusive lover, she knew the humiliation and baggage that came with being treated like you had no self-worth.

Velma glided the wide-bodied car into the trading post parking lot and continued beyond the front of the building, parking at the side where there was little traffic. "I paid cash for this car when I bought it and I plan to have it until I can no longer drive. I don't need some high or drunk kid running into it."

Shandra smiled. Aunt Jo had filled her in more and more about the family members. Velma was a throwback from her grandmother's generation. She believed in taking care of her things and not spending a penny more than was necessary. Which enlightened Shandra as to why Velma frowned every time she glanced at Shandra's fancy cowboy boots. To the woman, she squandered her money on fancy boots. But the dozen pair of fancy boots in Shandra's closet meant she'd arrived as an artist.

They both stopped inside the store doors. Shandra didn't have a clue who they were looking for. The return scowls and stares she and Velma received from the patrons and employees made her wonder if most of the population on the reservation were related to the Randal family.

"There he is, stocking the shelves." Velma marched by the checkout stations and down an aisle. A tall man in his twenties with two long braids and broad shoulders turned to them.

"Hi, Steve," Velma said, in a friendly tone.

"Hi, Velma." He eyed Shandra.

Paty Jager

"This is my cousin, Shandra Higheagle." Velma nodded to her.

"Hi, Steve. We have some questions to ask you about Saturday night at the lake." Shandra decided since he already looked anxious, she might as well let him know what they wanted.

"I've got nothing to say to you. I talked to the police." He turned back to the boxes stacked on the floor.

"You have to know there are at least four of you who would have stood up for Sandy." Instead of asking him about Coop, she'd decided to focus on Sandy, Arthur's victim.

He spun around, his face screwed up in anger. "Yeah, Arthur's lucky Coop got to him first. No girl deserves what Arthur done. But especially not Sandy."

She was beginning to wonder what was so special about this girl that had so many young men vying for her affection and standing up for her. "Why do you say that?"

"If I'd have gotten there first, he wouldn't have been able to walk away." The fury glinting in the young man's eyes showed her he had more of a temper than Coop.

"Maybe, you did make sure he didn't walk away?" she said softly for his ears only.

"No. I wish I had, but, no. When Sandy left and Coop followed, I snagged a bottle and a girl and left the lake."

"So if you can't have the one you love, love the one you're with?" She raised an eyebrow watching him.

"Something like that. Coop and Sandy are good together, but if he goes to jail, I'll make sure she has me to lean on."

An older woman in a faded house dress and well-worn athletic shoes shuffled up the aisle pushing a cart. Her rheumy gaze traveled the length of Shandra, over to Velma, and landed on Steve. "I need help," she said in a gravelly voice. "These two can help themselves."

"I'm coming, grama." Steve took a step toward the old woman.

Shandra grasped his arm. "What is the name of the girl you hooked up with?"

His eyes narrowed. "I told the others."

"But you didn't tell me." Her fingers remained gripped around his arm.

"Nelly Bingham."

She released his arm and turned to Velma. The older woman was tsking and shaking her head.

"What's wrong?" Shandra pulled out her list of names and added Nelly to the bottom.

"Rumors I've heard said Nelly had troubles with Arthur. Even if Steve wasn't with her when Arthur died, I would guess she will say she was." Velma jingled her keys and headed to the store entrance.

Having Velma along was a good thing. She knew something about everyone in the Agency and Nespelem.

In the car, Shandra pulled her phone out of her purse. "We need to know the time of death. It would be easier to ask people what were you doing at two a.m., than asking what they did after Coop beat up Arthur."

She hoped Liz would be forthcoming with this information. If not, she'd have to wait for Ryan to get a copy from his friend.

"Colville Confederated Tribes, Public Defender's Office," said the perky voice of the girl she'd met yesterday.

"Hello. This is Shandra Higheagle. If Ms. Piney isn't too busy, I'd like to speak with her, please."

"She's with a client. I can take your number and have her call you when she's finished."

Velma was pulling into the Ketch Pen parking lot. Shandra rattled off her number. "Thank you." She put her phone in her purse and studied her cousin. "What are we doing here?"

"This is where Dorsey spends his time when he's not at school and Billy Crow hangs out here most days." She tapped her fingers on the steering wheel. "So do a lot of people who were friends with Arthur."

That was a good reason to maybe try and talk to these two another time, but they were here and possibly one or both of the men were here, too.

She inhaled, grabbed her purse, and shoved the door open. Before she'd pushed the tavern door open, Velma was right behind her.

The dim lighting inside the door made her stop to get her bearings. Stale beer, fried food, and cigarette smoke assaulted her nose. She'd been in this establishment once before, when she was on the quest to discover how her father really died. The place looked much the same. Trios of lamps with variegated blue and green shades hung over the pool tables. A couple old men sat at the end of the bar. Several groups of men from their twenties to their fifties loitered around the pool tables. Some playing pool, others drinking and talking. A waitress stood by the bar, watching her and Velma. The same bartender as she'd gone a round with last time stood with his hands on the bar watching her.

"Let's sit down and you can see if Dorsey or Billy are here." Shandra walked over to the table closest to the pool tables that didn't have bottles. She studied the Indian artwork and alcohol ads on the walls while Velma stared at the groups of men.

"You two looking for something to drink or someone?" the waitress asked. She had on too much make-up, a sloppy shirt, and tight jeans stuffed into cowboy boots.

"I'll have coffee. I'm driving," Velma said.

Shandra studied the waitress, waiting impatiently. She didn't want to drink alcohol this early in the day, but she couldn't let the challenge in the woman's eyes go. "I'll have a beer."

The waitress's eyes widened in surprise before she spun away.

"And a glass," Shandra called after her. If she had to sip a beer, she wanted it in a glass and not a bottle.

Velma tapped her arm. "That one. In the blue plaid shirt. That's Billy Crow."

She studied the young man standing at the pool table the farthest from where they sat. Did she dare stroll over and try to start up a conversation? As if he felt her watching him, the man looked at her. A smile slid onto his lips, and he tipped his head slightly. Well, she'd caught his attention.

When the waitress returned she held out a ten. "Take the guy in the blue plaid shirt another of whatever he's drinking."

The woman raised her eyebrows but nodded. A few minutes later, she delivered a bottle of beer to Billy. He glanced over, raised the bottle in salute and took a long drink, watching her.

"You sure you want to give him more to drink?" Velma asked.

"No. But I'd rather he came to me than me get stuck in the middle of all those men."

"We should have sat at a table closer to the door." Velma raised her cup of coffee and clutched her purse to her body.

Shandra continued to make eye contact with Billy. He finished his game and it appeared his beer.

"I think he's looking for another free beer," Velma said, as the young man sauntered through the pool tables and stopped at their table.

"I could keep you company if you bought another round," he said, grasping the back of the chair at their table.

She could tell by his dilated pupils he probably shouldn't have another beer, but she had a feeling if he were sober he wouldn't be so easy to talk with her.

"Have a seat." She raised her hand. When the waitress looked her way she swirled her finger indicating to bring the people at her table another round of drinks.

The waitress brought the drinks, narrowing her

eyes, when she picked up Shandra's three-quarters full first beer bottle.

Billy took a long draw on his fresh beer and held out his hand. "I'm Billy."

Shandra grasped his hand. "I'm Shandra." When she tried to pull her hand back he continued to hold it.

"Your hands are rough for a woman who is dressed so fancy." He pulled her hand closer and stared at the palm.

"I'm a potter. Working with clay tends to dry out my hands." She extracted her hand from his. "What do you do?"

"I help my uncle when he needs it. Otherwise, I hang out here with my friends." He nodded toward the men playing pool. The men his age, who he'd been playing with, watched them.

"You like to party, Billy?" She caught Velma wiggling in her chair. A quick glance and the woman mouthed "restroom". She nodded and her cousin rose out of her chair and headed to the hallway with a restroom sign over the doorway.

"I'm glad she left." Billy leaned closer. His beer breath accosted her nose.

"Why?" She didn't want to flirt with the younger man, but she wasn't sure the best way to ask the questions that needed to be asked.

"I don't like the way she looks at me. It's like having my grandmother sitting at the table watching me make time with you." He made a face and took another long drink of beer.

She laughed. "Sorry. She's my cousin and

designated driver."

"You could send her home, and I could take you wherever you want to go."

"You have a car?" she asked, hoping to somehow get to the reason she was here.

"Yeah. A truck." He nodded and took another drink.

"You ever take your truck to parties?" She sipped her beer as Velma returned.

His eyes focused on her. "You like to party?"

"Sometimes. I like parties near water. Like a lake." She sipped again, not letting her gaze stray from his face. He didn't flinch.

"Yeah. We could take my truck and go party at a lake." He downed the rest of his beer.

She didn't want to go anywhere with him. But she'd feel better asking him the questions she wanted to ask out of sight of his friends.

"Sounds like fun." She sipped her beer and caught Velma shaking her head.

"Come on." He dug his hand into his pocket and pulled out a set of keys.

Shandra stood and followed him out of the bar. The bright June sunlight slapped them in the face, causing Billy to stop and Shandra to run into the back of him.

"Shit. That sun's bright," he said, wiping a hand across his eyes.

"It is summer," she said, scanning the vehicles in the parking lot and wondering which one belonged to him.

A hand touched her arm. She glanced over her

shoulder at Velma. The concern on the woman's face troubled her. She shook her head, trying to convey there wasn't anything to worry about.

"There's my truck." Billy weaved as he walked to the driver's side of a beat-up, green Chevy truck.

Shandra followed right behind him. When he grabbed the handle on the door and pulled, she leaned against the door.

"Billy, what can you tell me about Saturday night at Buffalo Lake?" She crossed her arms and studied him.

His face contorted from puzzled, to mad, to suspicious. "Why do you want to know?"

Chapter Eight

"I'm gathering information about what really happened at the lake this past Saturday. Do you think Coop really killed Arthur?" Shandra glimpsed Velma standing by her car, three trucks over.

Billy's lip curled up into a sneer. "Coop was mad as hell at Arthur." His face grew red. "That son-of-a-bitch hurt Sandy. I don't know what she was doing with him in the first place. She stays away from his type."

"I heard Arthur was interested in Sandy? Kind of like you, Steve, Dorsey, and Coop."

Billy's head snapped up. He stared at her with blood-shot eyes. "Sandy's got lots of friends because she doesn't talk bad about anyone, and she's working to get out of here. But she doesn't act better than the rest of us."

"Why would she go off alone with Arthur?"

"I don't know. She's smart enough to know better.

He could have snuck up on her." He rubbed a hand over his eyes. "Guys do that a lot at the parties. A girl goes to do her business in the bushes, and he sneaks up on her. But it's only in fun. You know, to scare her, make her scream. Then we laugh."

"When did you leave the party?" She needed to discover who was still at the lake when Arthur was killed.

"About an hour after Coop headed out after Sandy. The drinks were all gone. Everyone started getting in their cars and heading back." He leaned against the truck. "I guess you aren't going to the lake for a party."

She smiled. "No. Do you remember if Arthur had left the party?"

"His truck was still parked next to mine when I left." He pushed away from the vehicle. "I'm going back in."

"One more question. Had Coop returned to the party before you left?"

"No. He left right after he beat on Arthur. I didn't see either of them the rest of the weekend." He walked back to the door of the tavern.

Shandra walked over to Velma's car and slid into the passenger seat.

"Did you learn anything?"

"Yeah, so far no one seems to think Coop capable of killing anyone. And I can't wait to meet Sandy. Coop isn't the only one to put her on a pedestal." She buckled up as Velma backed the car out of the parking lot.

"Where are we going now?" She jotted down notes in her note pad.

"Find Dorsey." Velma accelerated down the highway.

"Tell me about Arthur? All I have so far is he seemed to have been a bully. Kind of like his grandfather."

Velma glanced over at her. "When have you met Oliver Randal?"

"Yesterday. After speaking to Liz, I thought I might catch Jo at the Community Center. But there was a mob of what appeared to be Randals, who were headed up by Oliver, rallying to go out looking for Coop."

"I heard about the gathering. I didn't know you were there." Her cousin shook her head. "It's a good thing they didn't know who you were."

"You mean Coop's cousin?"

"That and Aunt Minnie's granddaughter. The Randals don't like that some of us still believe in the Seven Drums."

Shandra stared at her cousin's profile. "I don't practice the Seven Drums religion."

"No, but word has spread that Aunt Minnie comes to you in dreams and you have powers."

Shandra shook her head. She didn't like the idea of anyone thinking she had powers or sight. "How could rumors like that have spread? The only people who know about the dreams are Aunt Jo and her family, and you." Narrowing her eyes, she stared at Velma. "Are you spreading the rumors?"

Her face took on a deeper hue. "No. But everyone knows how you solved your father's death. Many believe in your dreamer powers."

She laughed. It was ridiculous to say she had any powers. "I don't have powers other than deduction and help from a law enforcement officer."

They turned down a dirt road.

"Tell me about Arthur."

"He was a bully. Always has been, just like his grandfather. His father committed suicide when Arthur was a boy. He couldn't hold up to his father's bullying. Arthur's mother moved in with Oliver and his wife. The Randal men—Oliver, his sons, and Arthur and his cousins—all have tempers when they drink. And they take their resentments out on the women in the family."

Shandra stared at her cousin. "Don't they get in trouble for that?"

"Only if the woman is strong enough to call the cops or go to their family for help."

"So Arthur's treatment of Sandy is how he treats all women when he's drunk?" She had a hard time believing a young woman who had so many young men interested in her would have been dumb enough to be alone with Arthur at a party. "I would assume everyone knew of his drunken hatred of women?"

Velma nodded as she pulled the car up behind four vehicles that had seen better days. One appeared to have been rolled, the other had the side smashed in and two were up on blocks. The house was a small, one-story with faded blue paint and one window covered with plywood.

"This is where Dorsey lives?" Shandra asked, wondering how a young man living in this depressing house had found the strength and courage to go to college.

"Yes. His mother died when he was small and his father has been drunk most of his life." Velma smiled. "But Dorsey, even hanging out with Arthur, has managed to do well in school and your cousin, Theodore, helped him apply for scholarships to attend Whitworth College in Spokane. He was accepted, and from what Theodore says, is doing quite well."

Shandra stepped out of the car. She waited for Velma to reach her before they both walked up to the faded wood door. The creak of the porch steps started a dog barking in the house.

"Shut up!" shouted a slurred voice.

"Aldon, it's Velma Wilber," her cousin called.

"Go away!" he shouted back.

"We can't. We need to speak to Dorsey." Velma grasped the door knob and smiled when it turned.

Stepping behind her large cousin, Shandra hoped the man was dressed. She didn't want to see a half-dressed drunk.

Her cousin shoved the door open. "Aldon, pull that blanket over your lap!" She didn't go any farther than the doorway, blocking the view, which was fine with Shandra.

"Why are all you big women bossy?" the man asked.

"Because we know little men like you need bossing." Velma stepped forward.

Shandra remained on the porch. The sweat, urine, and stale beer fumes that wafted out the door helped to glue her feet to the outside stoop.

"Where's Dorsey?" Velma asked, again.

"He hasn't been here in days." A belch echoed his statement.

"Where does he go when he's not here?" Her cousin was persistent as a blood hound.

"He goes to Arthur's."

"Arthur's dead."

There was a moment of silence before the man chuckled. "I told Dorsey that little shit would try to push the wrong person one day."

Shandra stepped across the threshold.

The man's gaze rested on her. He grinned showing missing teeth. "Minnie, I knew you hadn't left us."

She glanced over at Velma. The woman smiled and nodded. She didn't know what her cousin wanted her to do.

"I told'em at the Ketch Pen you wouldn't leave us."

"I'm not Minnie, I'm Shandra, Minnie's granddaughter." Shandra took two more steps into the room.

"Dorsey's a good boy. I told him not to be hanging around with them Randals." He set the beer can down and slicked his hair back with a hand. "I tried to keep him out of trouble after his mother passed."

"Aldon. You have a good boy. Get sober and make him proud of you." Velma grabbed Shandra's shoulders, turning her, and ushered her toward the door.

Outside, as they stood by the car, Velma inhaled several large breaths of fresh air.

"Do we go to the Randals?" Shandra asked.

"No. We get lunch, then go see Sandy. And we get her to call Dorsey and get him to come to us." Velma grinned and slid in behind the steering wheel.

"I like the way you think." Shandra settled into the passenger seat as her phone played a jazz tune.

Chapter Nine

Shandra glanced at her phone. It was Liz. "Hi Liz. Thanks for calling me back."

"What did you need?" the public defender asked.

"Is there a chance I could get the time of death on Arthur Randal?"

There was a moment of silence.

"Why do you need to know that?" The suspicion in her voice told Shandra she wouldn't be able to get this woman's help as easily as she did from Ryan.

"I'd like to know. Andy and I have been putting together a timeline. He's been talking to friends about when they left the lake." She glanced at Velma. The woman was grinning like she had a triple scoop ice cream cone in her hand.

"We, the public defender's office, will talk with everyone and take their statements. Lawfully. Does this have anything to do with you and Velma driving around asking questions?"

She sucked in air. How did the woman know they were asking questions?

"That's what I thought. Who have you talked to so far?"

"Steve Wood and Billy Crow."

Velma let out a disgusted sigh as if she'd let the older woman down by giving in so fast.

The sound of paper flipping came through the phone.

"Why those two?" Liz asked.

"They both have a thing for Sandy. I figure whoever killed Arthur did it out of revenge for what he did to Sandy, so that means the young men who like her are the prime suspects." She was proud of her deduction.

"But that would put Coop right back in the pot. He was the only one to stand up for her." Liz had a point.

"True. But he left to catch Sandy and from what I can gather from the two I've talked to, that as long as Coop's in the picture, they consider Sandy hands off. But if he were framed for a murder and sent away, they would be only too happy to jump in and stand up for Sandy. It's a weird kind of respect for another guy's girl, but the minute he's gone, they'd move in like vultures."

"It's respect for another's property."

That irked. "No woman should be any man's property." This was a button that once pushed with her, she had a hard time letting go. She'd been a woman who'd been a man's property and she'd not let that happen again.

"I agree. But that's the way the men here think. They respect their women, but they are their women." A knock on a door and voices came through the line. "I have to go. Don't get close to the Randals. They are out for blood with this."

The line went dead. Shandra shoved her phone into her purse.

"You have something you want to tell me?" Velma asked.

"No. Let's get that lunch and go see Sandy."

~*~

Shandra managed to keep Velma from asking any more questions about her screwed up years at college. They drove to a neat and tidy house in the middle of Nespelem. The color was neutral. A small flower bed had brightly colored blooms. A compact car sat in the drive.

"That's Sandy's. She should be home." Velma stepped out of the car and walked up to the door.

"Coop said he dropped her off at her cousin's on Saturday. Could she be there?" Shandra asked as Velma rapped on the door.

"She could. It's only a few houses over. She could have walked." The older woman had an annoyed furrow in her brow. She rapped on the door several more times. "Give me your phone."

Shandra handed over her phone.

Velma punched in a number, listened, and then said, "This is Velma. Is Sandy there visiting Ruby?"

She listened. "Is she home?" Her eyes narrowed and her brows nearly touched. "Why would her mother let her do that?" She listened and handed the phone back.

"Who was that?" Shandra asked, turning her phone off and shoving it into her purse.

"Ruby's mother, Sandy's aunt. She said Sandy's mother sent her to a cousin in Omak." Velma marched to the car, slamming the door when she sat behind the wheel.

"I don't understand." Shandra slid into the passenger seat and closed the door. "Why would she send her daughter away? She didn't kill Arthur…" Her mind flashed to the anger she'd felt against Carl, the man who'd undermined her faith in herself. Sandy could have gone out after Coop left her at Ruby's and taken care of the man who'd assaulted her.

"We need to know how Arthur was killed." If he'd been drunk enough, it would have been easy for an angry woman to hold his head under water and drown him. Even slug him in the head with a rock.

"How are we going to talk to Dorsey without someone to lure him to us?" Velma asked.

"We'll ask Ruby to call Dorsey. Say Sandy wants to talk to him." She liked this, but would have rather talked to Sandy. "Maybe we can get a number to contact Sandy while we talk to Ruby."

Velma started the car and roared out of the driveway and down the street a couple blocks. She turned left and pulled into a house not as neat and tidy as the last, but a lot better than the house Dorsey grew up in.

Before Shandra could get her door open, Velma was marching up to the house. The door opened and a woman a little bit younger than Velma, but older than herself, stood in the doorway. She didn't have a welcoming smile on her face.

"I knew you'd be showing up here. I could tell by your voice. What do you want?"

"We'd like to talk to Ruby," Velma said.

Ruby's mother studied Shandra. "Who is she?"

"My cousin. Shandra Higheagle."

"Edward's daughter?" The woman's eyes widened. She leaned toward Shandra. "You here to help Coop?"

"Yes. That's why we need to speak to Ruby."

"Ruby wasn't at the party. She was working." The woman straightened and drew her shoulders back as if she planned to defend her home and daughter.

"We know that. But Sandy may have told her something that could help us prove Coop didn't do it." Appealing to this mother to help another the age of her daughter seemed like the way to get her help.

"And we need her to call Dorsey and get him here so we can talk to him," Velma said, pushing her way by the other woman.

"Looks like I have no choice." Ruby's mother stepped back and let her enter.

Velma had already taken the nicest chair in the living room. "Bring Ruby on out here," she said.

Shandra tried to appear apologetic for Velma's rudeness. "We really need to speak to Ruby. Sandy could have told her something."

The woman studied her a minute then hollered,

"Ruby!"

A teenaged girl sauntered into the living room from the hallway. She stopped at the sight of Velma. The woman had an interesting effect on people. One that she planned to look into after Coop was free.

"Ruby, I'm Shandra Higheagle, Coop's cousin."

"The artist! I saw one of your vases in a magazine at school." Ruby sat on the arm of the upholstered chair next to Shandra, completely ignoring Velma.

"Are you studying art?" she asked, hoping to make the girl feel comfortable with her.

"No, just took a pottery class." She skimmed a bare toe back and forth across the matted carpet.

"We need to know what Sandy said to you on Saturday when Coop dropped her off and if you saw Coop any time after that." Velma moved a bit in her peripheral vision. She hoped the woman would remain quiet and let her deal with the girl.

"Sandy was upset. She said Arthur had snuck up on her when she was peeing. She managed to get her pants up and zipped before he grabbed her." The girl's eyes glimmered with anger. "I'm glad Coop beat him up. He's always picking on the girls. Hurting them when they don't want him touching them."

"So he was known to be mean to girls?"

"Yeah. We all knew to stay away from him. Especially when he was drinking. That always made him worse." She glanced over her shoulder at her mother. "That's what girls said. I wouldn't know."

Shandra smiled. "Did Sandy say anything about Coop?"

"She said he showed her he was the only one who cared enough about her to do something." Her gaze became soft and dreamy. "There's days I wish I was older and Coop saw me as more than Sandy's cousin."

Her cousin had a long list of hearts he could capture it appeared. But he had eyes for Sandy. "So she was grateful for Coop beating up Arthur?"

"Yeah, she said it was about time someone stood up to him."

"Did she say if Arthur said anything to her?" Shandra wondered about Arthur picking Sandy as his victim that night. Had it been random or specific?

"Something about showing him some of what she showed Dorsey." The girl's brow wrinkled in puzzlement. "I don't understand what he meant? Sandy only ever kissed Coop. But she was nice to everyone."

Shandra understood the younger woman's puzzlement. Sandy must not have liked Arthur, and with good reason, yet, had been nice to Dorsey, which angered the bully.

"I have two favors to ask of you. Could you give me Sandy's phone number so I can call and ask her some things about Coop? And would you call Dorsey and tell him Sandy is here and would like to talk to him?" Shandra hoped Ruby would do both.

"Just a minute." She hurried down the hall and returned with her phone. Scrolling through her contacts she held the phone up for Shandra to write down Sandy's number.

"I don't have Dorsey's number." She thought a moment. "But Elsie might. Hold on." She scrolled the

73

contacts again and tapped the screen.

Shandra touched her arm. "Don't tell her why you need it. Word gets around here fast enough."

The girl nodded and stepped into the dining area.

Shandra walked over to Velma. "You might want to park your car a block or so away. We don't want to scare off Dorsey."

Ruby came back to the living room. "Dorsey is on his way. He didn't even ask why she wanted to see him." Her grin encompassed her whole face.

Velma moved to the door. "Do you want me to stay away until you're done talking to him?"

Shandra heard the hurt in her cousin's voice, but she did tend to rub people the wrong way. "If you don't mind?"

Velma nodded and marched out the door.

Ruby and her mother both sighed at the same time.

"What is it about Velma that everyone seems to be on edge around her?" she asked the mother and daughter.

"Velma sees things. It makes most of us uneasy to be with her. She says she knows this or that." Ruby's mother glanced at her daughter.

Secrets. It appeared Velma knew others secrets and let them know. Shandra faced Ruby. "Did Coop come back here later? After he dropped Sandy off?"

Ruby nodded. "I think so. I didn't see him, but I heard what sounded like his truck, slow down and idle."

"What about Sandy? Did she say if she saw him later?" Shandra had to find someone to corroborate Coop's statement that he came back by here before staying with his friend. Who she needed to talk to as well.

"I don't know. After she cleaned up and put on one of my shirts, she went home." The girl shrugged.

Shandra was shuffling this new information around when the roar of a motor and screeching of brakes penetrated the walls.

Banging on the door shot Ruby's mother across the room. She pulled the door open.

A tall, wide shouldered, young man stood in the doorway. His shoulder-length hair hid the outside half of his eyes. He shoved the hair out of his face as he strode into the room.

"Where's Sandy?" he asked.

Shandra stepped forward, her hand extended. "She's not here. I had Ruby call and invite you here."

He stared at her hand.

"I'm Shandra Higheagle, Coop's cousin."

His gaze shot to her face. "Coop's cousin. Why would I want to talk to you?"

"To help Sandy." She knew he'd never help Coop.

"Why would Sandy need help? Coop killed Arthur." His glare dared her to say otherwise.

"I don't think Coop did. Everyone knows he doesn't have it in him to take a life. To beat up someone who hurt the woman he loves, yes."

The young man flinched at the mention of Coop loving Sandy. He was jealous.

"I saw Coop walking away from the party with Arthur." Again, his eyes dared her to say he lied.

"You couldn't have. Coop didn't return to the party

after bringing Sandy here." She crossed her arms. "But *you* could have walked Arthur to the dock and killed him. I think you care more about Sandy than your lifelong pal."

His gaze wavered a minute.

"I think you said it was Coop to get him out of Sandy's life. I don't think you killed your friend. But I bet you were mad at how he'd treated Sandy."

"He knew to keep his hands off her. I'd told him whenever he said something about taking that snooty bitch down a peg or two that he'd have to answer to me if he touched her." He shoved the hair that had fallen back across his eyes out of the way.

"Why'd he go against your wishes at the party?" There had to be a reason Arthur had assaulted Sandy.

"He was mad when Coop arrived. He and Lyle have been eating at Arthur since the basketball tournament. He said they'd rigged it so the ref called everything on us and made us lose."

She shook her head. It was hard to believe someone would be that bent up about a basketball game. "I heard your team had been physically beating up the other teams. That when you got a ref that wouldn't put up with it you lost."

His gaze dropped to the floor. He knew his team had played unfairly and been beaten fairly.

"So to get Coop to leave, he attacked Sandy? Seems a bit childish."

"You gotta know Arthur. His grandpa has put all kinds of things in his mind about people." Dorsey's face darkened. "But he went too far hurting Sandy."

Ruby stood up from where she'd been perched on the chair arm. "Why did he tell Sandy to give him some of what she gave you?"

His face turned to stone as she'd seen so many on this reservation do when they wanted to hide their feelings.

"What did you tell Arthur about Sandy?" Shandra asked softly.

They all jolted at sharp rapping on the door. Ruby hurried across the room and opened the door.

Shandra groaned.

Chapter Ten

Shandra stared at the blond-haired man in a black suit. Agent Weatherly. What would he say about her talking to the person who incriminated her cousin?

The agent's gaze traveled from person to person, landing on her. His eyes narrowed. He pulled his badge from the inside of his suit coat.

"Agent Weatherly of the FBI. I've been looking for you, Dorsey." He glanced at the young man and then at Ruby's mother. "I'm also looking for Sandy Williams. I was told she might be here."

Ruby's mother stepped forward. "Sandy isn't here. She's staying with another aunt."

"I'll be going," Shandra said, walking by Ruby and giving her a pat on the arm.

"I'll step outside with you," Agent Weatherly said. He pointed a finger at Dorsey. "You stay put until I come back."

Shandra headed out the door and scanned the streets, hoping Velma was waiting somewhere close. She wasn't.

"What are you doing here?"

She swung around and nearly bumped into the FBI agent. "Talking." She took several steps back from the man. He stood a good six foot if not a couple inches more. He didn't have broad shoulders, but she'd bet he was athletic.

"Talking to two of my witnesses. Why is it, you seem to be a step ahead of me everywhere I've been today?" He crossed his arms, standing like a statue in front of her.

She wished he didn't have on dark glasses. With the colored lenses covering his eyes, she couldn't tell his exact emotions.

"I don't know what you're talking about. I'm here visiting my aunt and cousins."

He nodded toward the house they'd both just stepped out of. "Is someone in there a relation to you?"

"No, but I came here with my cousin who knows them." Her excuse was lame, but it was the truth.

"And where is this cousin? I only saw Mrs. Perkins, Ruby, and Dorsey Flint." He continued to stand still as stone.

"She offered to run to the store." A vehicle moving down the gravel street caught her attention. It was Velma. "There she is. I need to go."

He stepped in front of her. "I thought she ran to the store. She'll need to bring whatever she purchased to Mrs. Perkins."

Her cheeks grew warm as the man stood his ground.

"Here I am. Why are you out here? Can't have tea and cookies with you standing out here." Velma marched up beside her, grabbed her arm, and led her back in the house. Her other hand had a white plastic bag.

"I'm glad to see you," she whispered to her cousin as they walked through the open front door.

"Here I am, just like I said. And here's the cookies. Gladys put some water on for tea." Velma glared at Dorsey, but shoved him into a chair at the dining room table before turning to Agent Weatherly, who had followed them into the house. "Are you staying for tea and cookies?"

He pulled off his sunglasses and stared pointedly at both Velma and herself. "I don't know who you are, but I want both of you to leave."

"That's unhospitable of you considering we was invited and you wasn't," Velma said, ramming her fisted hands on her ample hips.

Agent Weatherly pointed to the door and poked his finger at first Velma and then Shandra. "You and you. Go. Before I have you arrested for obstructing justice."

Shandra walked to the door. "Come on, Velma. We know when we're not wanted." She smiled at Mrs. Perkins, Ruby, and Dorsey. "Sorry we can't stay. It was nice meeting you."

Her mind wanted her to run to the car, but she kept her steps even. She heard Velma huffing behind her. They both slid into the car and didn't say a word until the tires hummed on the highway pavement.

"How did you know I told him you were at the store?" Shandra was still surprised her cousin had shown up at the house with a bag of cookies.

"I had a suspicion he'd show up there after talking to Steve at the trading post and he told me the agent had been asking him several of the same questions you asked." Velma shot her a big grin. "So, I bought the cookies hoping you'd say I ran an errand and was coming back for you." She tapped her temple. "Great minds think alike."

Shandra laughed, wishing she'd connected with this side of her family much sooner. If she'd had the chance to get to know them when she was younger, she would have left her mother and step-father and lived here. And that was exactly why her mother kept her from her father's people.

"I need to call Sandy before Agent Weatherly gets the number from Ruby." She pulled the slip of paper with the number out of her pocket.

"You can call at my house." Velma turned her car down the road leading to her house. "I have more cookies in the back seat." She chuckled, turning her car into the driveway.

In the house, Shandra sat at the table while Velma made tea and coffee and placed the cookies she'd bought on a plate.

With the phone number spread out on the table, Shandra tapped the screen and listen to the sound of the phone ringing.

"Hello?" questioned a soft female voice.

"Sandy?"

"Yes. Who is this?"

"I'm Shandra Higheagle, Co—"

"Oh, I'm so glad you're here! Coop told me about you. If anyone can help him, it's you." The young woman's voice wavered toward the end.

"I plan to help him. That's why I'm calling. Can you tell me everything you remember about Saturday night?"

A strangled sob floated through the phone. The sound of a door closing followed.

"You don't have to tell me any more than you feel comfortable about. What I need to know is what happened after you and Coop left the lake." She felt Velma's gaze on her. "I'm also a very good listener."

"Like Coop." Sandy sighed. "I know he didn't kill Arthur. I don't care what Dorsey says. Coop would never do that."

"I agree. What happened?" Shandra picked up a cookie and nibbled. Velma took a seat across the table from her.

"Arthur must have seen me go out into the bushes to take a pee. I'd just got my pants up and he grabbed me from behind. A hand over my mouth so no one heard my scream." Her angry tone reflected what she thought of his actions. "I didn't think he'd…you know." Her voice faltered. "He asked me what I saw in Coop. I told him. He laughed. Said he had a notion to tell Coop I was two-timing because he saw me with Dorsey when Coop was at school. It's not what he thought." The conviction in her voice was genuine.

"Dorsey and I take the same class. I've been helping him, like a tutor. I helped him get through school and get that scholarship. I wanted him to get away from Arthur and his family. But he has some weird loyalty to them." She inhaled. "When I told him there was nothing between Dorsey and I, he said, 'yeah, sure. I want what you give him.' That's when he tried to kiss me. I shoved him away. He grabbed my shirt, ripping it and swinging his hand at the same time, slapping me." She choked out the last part.

"I'm sorry you had to deal with him. I never met Arthur, but he sounds like a man I spent some time with. You have a good man in Coop. He'll help you." Shandra thought of Carl, her deceased ex-lover. She'd willingly allowed his mistreatment until she'd become wiser. Sandy was young and her encounter was a one-time thing. With someone as caring as Coop by her side, she'd get over the trauma. Just like Ryan had helped her overcome her fears of being close with a man.

"We have to get him out of jail," Sandy said on a rushed breath.

"I heard he is up for arraignment on Friday. I'll post his bail then, but he'll have to stay at the ranch so he doesn't get cornered by the Randals." Shandra had thought about not posting his bail and leaving him where he was safe. But Aunt Jo and Sandy needed him home.

"I can meet you in court on Friday," Sandy offered.

"That's a good idea." Shandra shifted her thoughts back to what she needed to know. "After Coop beat up

Arthur and he caught up to you, what happened on the way back to the agency?"

"I was a mess. I didn't want my mom to see my clothes and I was crying. Coop had his arm around me all the way back." She paused. "Except when he realized Andy was in the back of the pickup. He made him get out and told him to find a ride back."

"Did Coop stay with you at Ruby's?" She knew the answer but hoped the woman didn't try to give Coop an alibi.

"No. I told him we'd talk later. He said he was going to go back and get Andy." She inhaled. "Oh God! That isn't going to sound good."

"It's fine. That's what he told me. Coop didn't find Andy but talked to a Lyle…"

"Oh! That's Coop's best friend. Lyle Near. I bet the two of them drove back together. That's where he spent the night."

"Coop said he tried to see you again, but you weren't at Ruby's."

"He did? I went home after I changed, washed my face, and applied some makeup. Didn't he ask Ruby? She would have told him."

"He could have called you and asked where you were. Did he?" That would account for Ruby thinking she heard his truck idling in the street.

"I… my phone was in my car at the lake."

"But you have it now." Shandra's mind raced with thoughts of Sandy sneaking back and striking…no she didn't know how Arthur died. Her next call would be to see if Ryan came through with an autopsy report.

"Butch, my brother, found it after I left. He gave it to me the next morning." There was no hesitation.

"Is your brother older or younger than you?" She wondered at his being at a party with his sister. But Andy and Coop had both been at the same party. How many people attended parties at the lake?

"He's younger by three years."

"Neither one of you are drinking age," she said.

Velma snorted, spewing coffee over the cookie she held in her other hand.

"Well, no one really cares here. Everyone drinks."

Shandra wasn't taking that for an answer. "I don't believe everyone drinks. Many do, but not everyone. That's not a good excuse." Oh man, now I sound like an old person!

"I don't drink much. Coop usually finishes off his and mine, then we put water in the bottles." She paused. "He said he can't mess up or he won't get his degree. He wants me to be successful too."

"I'm glad my cousin has good sense." She picked up the tea Velma slid in front of her. "When you come for the arraignment on Friday, you should sit down with Coop's attorney and tell her everything you've told me."

"I will. I promise." Her breathy promise was all Shandra needed.

"See you Friday." She tapped the phone off and sipped her tea.

"What did you find out?" Velma asked, before biting into another cookie.

"We have another suspect."

Chapter Eleven

Shandra waited until she was back at her aunt and uncle's ranch and curled up ready for bed before calling Ryan. She'd made notes about what she'd learned during the day.

She picked up the phone to call and jazz music filled the air. A glance at the image on the phone made her smile. Ryan. She swiped the screen with her finger.

"Hello. I was just getting ready to call you."

"Then it was good timing." His deep masculine voice filled her with comfort.

"How was your day?" she asked, not jumping right into what she wanted to ask.

"The usual. My friend in the FBI sent me what they have so far on your cousin's case."

Her heart thumped against her ribs. She hoped the results would help her narrow down the list of suspects she had so far. But not wanting Ryan to hear how important that information was to her, she said, "Oh, good. What was the usual?"

He laughed. "You can try to be casual all you want. I hear how excited you are to get these results."

She laughed. "I didn't want you to think I was only calling you for that."

"Word is, your name has already made it to the FBI headquarters in Spokane. Just exactly what have you been up to today?"

"Agent Weatherly feels intimidated by Velma and me." She laughed and went on to tell him who she'd talked to and what she'd learned. "So I need to know how Arthur was killed and time of death to narrow down my list of suspects."

"Your cousin in the Public Defender's Office wouldn't help you?"

She heard the reproach in his voice. "Not so much wouldn't help as wanted me to keep from getting into trouble."

"That I can understand. You didn't get this from me or my friend."

"I know. I'll say Velma 'saw' the results. Everyone here is scared of her because she 'sees' things."

"Your sidekick today?" Humor had inched back into his voice.

"Yeah, my sidekick who doesn't completely approve of me." Again she was overwhelmed by the way her family had welcomed her back. "I'd wished today that I had been a part of this family since childhood." Her voice caught on the lump of emotion clogging her throat.

"If that had happened you most likely wouldn't have gone to college and become the artist you are today. Or have had the ability to help Coop right now," he said softly. "How we live is what shapes us. If you hadn't gone through what you have, you wouldn't be the strong woman you are now."

He spoke the truth.

"You're going to make me cry." She sniffed, wishing she could fold into his arms and feel his strength. A strength she'd come to rely on heavily the last few months.

"I'll change the subject." His voice was raspy with emotion. "Arthur Randal died of blunt force trauma to the back of his head and died between one and three a.m."

She sighed. "That's a big gap. And so far, I haven't found anyone who could say for sure Coop wasn't at the lake then." A thought struck her. "I don't even know what time he and Sandy left."

"It looks like you need to make a timeline." He paused. "I have time off coming. I plan to join you on Friday if you aren't coming back."

Excitement and apprehension rivaled. She was excited he was coming to help, but worried his presence would keep people from talking to her. It helped to have Velma with her when she talked to everyone. Having another outsider with her would close mouths. "I'd love for you to come. However, I'll have to continue talking to people with Velma along. They would never talk to the two of us. I'm lucky Velma scares them all into talking." She laughed halfheartedly.

"I understand. But I would like to be there for support."

"Then I'd love for you to come."

"I'll see you Friday, and call you again tomorrow night." Longing deepened Ryan's voice.

"I'll look forward to your call." She smiled and tapped the screen, ending the conversation.

"Andy!" she called, knowing her cousin was in his room across the hall.

"Yeah?" He grabbed the door jamb to stop his forward momentum.

"I need times." She pulled out her notepad. "What time did Coop and Sandy leave the party?"

"Eleven-thirty. Maybe later. I know it was before midnight." He stepped into the room and sat in the desk chair. "You learn something new?"

"Yes. What time did you get picked up on the road?"

"After midnight. We didn't get back to the agency until one. Then I had to catch a ride out here."

"And you didn't see your brother at all in that time?"

"Nope. Once he ditched me, I didn't see him until I found him hiding in the barn and helped him camp in the hills." He leaned forward, his forearms on his legs. She'd witnessed his brother sit in much the same way. "Are we going to be able to prove Coop didn't do this?"

"Yes. It just takes talking to the right people and finding the clues." She tapped her notepad. "Do you know Nelly Bingham?"

Paty Jager

Andy's face flushed a deeper tone. "Why?"

"She's Steve Wood's alibi. I haven't talked to her yet, but Velma said she and Arthur had bad feelings." Shandra watched her cousin. She could see him puzzling things in his head.

"She accused Arthur of attacking her a while back. Nothing came of it because she gets around if you know what I mean." His left eyebrow rose.

"Even if she sleeps around, no one should be allowed to hurt her." Shandra didn't care who the woman was, they didn't deserve to be treated like they had no worth.

"I agree. But after Arthur's grandfather spread rumors she dropped her accusations." Andy shrugged.

"What has that man got on people that they follow him like lemmings and do his bidding?" She was starting to think if she didn't find solid evidence soon, Oliver Randal would railroad Coop into jail even though he'd not committed a crime.

"He's loud and makes people believe his way of thinking is the right way."

She shook her head. "It's not. I also need to talk to Lyle, Coop's friend." She glanced at the time on her phone. "Is it too late to go see him?"

Andy stood. "Nope. He's probably at his sister's. Her and her husband live between here and Nespelem."

Shandra picked up her notepad and phone, shoving them into her purse. "I'll get dressed and we can to see Lyle.

She dressed and met up with Andy at the bottom of the stairs. She tossed her keys to him. "You drive."

In the kitchen, Aunt Jo stopped them. "Where are you two going? It's after nine."

"I'm taking Shandra to talk to Lyle." Andy dangled her keys, making them jingle.

"Coop said Lyle saw him when he returned to the lake looking for Andy. I have some questions for him." Shandra wanted to clear up a couple of things others had said.

Jo's face lit up. "Those two have been friends a long time. He'll help clear my boy." She waved them toward the door. "Go. The sooner this is cleared up, the better."

Andy kissed his mother on the cheek as he walked by. "Don't worry. We'll get him home and back to school."

Shandra followed her cousin to the Jeep. Inside, she turned to him. "That was nice of you to give your mom support." Every time she stayed with this family she wished things had been different and she had had siblings and parents who cared about her and not their status.

"It's true. You're going to figure this out, and Coop will be free to finish school and marry Sandy." He backed the Jeep and drove down the road.

"Do you think he'll ask Sandy to marry him?" She knew Coop was infatuated with the girl, but if she was so friendly with so many other young men, she might not be a good choice for her cousin. And I still haven't ruled her out as a suspect.

"Oh, he'll ask her." He hesitated, his attention on the road. "I'm not positive she'll say yes."

"That's my thought, too." She huffed, sending her doubts into the evening air. "We have to clear him and worry about the rest later."

Andy nodded.

"Tell me about Lyle." She'd learned from her experiences today that knowing a person before meeting them gave her an edge on how to ask questions.

"He and Coop have been friends since grade school. He's even more athletic than Coop. The two of them can beat anyone on the reservation at basketball."

"The reason Arthur was mad at Coop and took it out on Sandy," she said, remembering her conversation with Dorsey.

"What are you talking about?"

She relayed what Dorsey had told her about Arthur being upset over the basketball tournament.

"That's why he ripped Sandy's shirt? To get back at Coop for winning?" He said a few expletives under his breath and muttered, "That's lame."

"I agree."

The sun was dipping lower in the west, casting the world into the gray of dusk, as Andy swung the Jeep down a dirt road off the main highway. Several houses, some in need of repairs and some in livable conditions, were scattered along the road. He turned into the drive of a small, single-story, ranch-style house.

Droopy flowers in need of water lined the dirt walkway to the porch. A pair of wicker chairs sat on the porch with a small table between them.

Shandra followed Andy up the walkway.

"Woof! Woof!" A dog loped around the side of the house. He was a bit larger than Sheba with a short tan coat and a wrinkled black face, slobbering drool.

"My you're a big boy," Shandra said, holding her hand out.

"Watch yourself. That's Lyle's dog. He's not too friendly." Andy had scrambled up on the porch and rapped on the door.

"He's a good dog." She patted the dog's massive head and was positive he smiled. "You and my dog, Sheba, would have a fun time together." She scratched behind the dog's ears.

Andy knocked on the door again. "They're always home."

A young man Coop's age strode around the side of the house. "Who—?" His gaze landed on Andy. "Hey, little brother, what are you doing here?" He walked up to the dog and put a hand on his back. "And who have you brought for a visit?"

Shandra smiled and held out her hand. "Shandra Higheagle. Andy and Coop's cousin."

He shook hands. "Coop told me about you. In fact, I saw you at the community center the last time you were here."

Thinking back, she did remember him. He was one of the boys with her cousins when she'd stopped in to see Aunt Jo her first trip back after her grandmother's funeral. "I remember. Pleased, to meet you."

"I see you've met Horse."

Shandra laughed. "Horse? That's what you call this mighty dog?"

93

Lyle laughed. "Yeah, he's big enough you could ride him. In fact, my nieces and nephews do."

Andy walked over and joined them. "Shandra wanted to ask you some questions. She's trying to prove Coop didn't kill Arthur."

Lyle's eyelids dropped to half-mast, hiding whatever emotion reflected in them. "Not much I can help you with."

"Did you see the fight between Coop and Arthur?" She decided after witnessing his rapid change of mood, she'd ease into the main thing she wanted to ask.

"Yes. Coop could have kicked Arthur's ass more. But he's too nice."

"I think he wanted to teach Arthur a lesson and get Sandy out of there," Shandra suggested.

"Yeah. After he knocked Arthur to the ground, he told me he was taking Sandy home and asked me to give you," he punched Andy in the shoulder, "a ride."

"I tagged along with Coop and Sandy." Her cousin grinned. "I jumped in the back of the truck."

"That's why I couldn't find you when I was ready to leave. I asked everyone where you were, and no one knew, so I left."

"What time was that?" Shandra asked.

"That I left the lake?" he asked, stalling.

"Yes. What time did you leave the lake?" She continued to pet the dog but had her attention fully on the young man.

"I'm not sure. The beer had run out. I'd asked everyone getting in their trucks if they'd seen Andy." He transferred his weight to one foot, cocking his right knee. "Must have been after one."

"Did you happen to see if Arthur's truck was still there?" She wanted to make sure Billy Crow had told her the truth, though she believed anyone as drunk as he was wouldn't have had the sharpness to lie.

"Yeah. I remember seeing it as Billy Crow left. It was parked by his."

"Do you remember seeing Coop headed back to the lake?" Shandra asked.

"Yeah. I stopped and he asked if I'd seen you." He pointed to Andy. "I said no and no one was left at the lake."

"You were the last one to leave, but Arthur's truck was still there?" Shandra watched him closely. With him being the last person to leave the lake besides Arthur, he could have bashed the other man's head in with a rock.

His eyes narrowed. "Hey. I didn't kill him. Don't try saying I did to get Coop off."

"I'm not. I'm gathering all the information." She stared in his eyes. "You're sure you didn't see anyone else around when you left?"

He shook his head. "I asked everyone as they left if they'd seen Andy."

"But you didn't think it was strange that Arthur's truck was still at the lake?"

"No. People hook up or drink so much they can't drive and catch rides with other people. Sandy's car was still there. Coop took her home. I figured after his beating, Arthur had Dorsey drive him home."

"Were there any other cars besides those two?"

95

When had Sandy gone back and retrieved her car? That night and found Arthur drunk and easy to retaliate against? Coop wouldn't like where her thoughts and inquiries were taking her.

Lyle crossed his arms and appeared to be deep in thought. "I don't think so."

"Did Nelly Bingham drive to the party by herself?" Steve had said he'd hooked up with Nelly. If so, where was her car?

Lyle frowned. "I don't keep tabs on her."

"Steve Woods said he took her with him when the beer ran out." Nelly was definitely the first person she was going to talk to tomorrow. Along with contacting Liz to ask about Arthur's truck.

Lyle laughed. "He picked up Nelly 'cause Sandy left with Coop."

She studied the young man. "You and Coop know about Steve's crush on Sandy?"

"Hell yeah. It's a good thing Coop ain't the jealous kind. Sandy has guys falling all over themselves for her." He slammed his fist into his palm. "But who stuck up for her when Arthur harassed her?"

"The one who would stick up for anyone being threatened." Shandra shook her head. Coop's chivalry could very well be the thing that would make it hard to find the real killer.

Chapter Twelve

Shandra drifted off to sleep with all the people she'd talked to that day spinning in her head. The two things on her mind were: How did Sandy get her car back and how to prove when Coop went back to look for Andy that he hadn't continue on to the lake and encountered Arthur. Her biggest fear was discovering the killer was Sandy.

Coyotes howled to the growing June moon. She rolled to her side, watching the play of moonlight on the trees, bushes, and rocks on the hills outside. The breeze through her open window filled the room with the scent of horses. As a child she'd loved laying on the hay in the barn, staring up at the rafters, listening to the animals, and inhaling the scent of horse, hay, and leather.

She closed her eyes and pretended she was in that barn. It was one of the few things growing up her mother hadn't harassed her about. She'd understood Shandra's love of horses.

She drifted to sleep, listening to the sound of horses hooves.

Grandmother sat on the top rail of a wooden corral. She waved her arm, drawing Shandra near. "What is it Ella?" she asked, climbing up beside her grandmother.

The fence hadn't felt tall when she climbed up but now she looked down and saw small horses grazing in a field. "Why...?" she started to ask about the distance when a small cloud drifted by. They were sitting on a fence in the sky.

Ella pointed downward. A man on a horse herded other horses to the pasture. He cut the fence and chased the horses in.

"Is that a Randal?" Shandra asked.

Grandmother nodded.

"Why are you showing me what happened so long ago? It can't have anything to do with the murder."

Sadness filled her grandmother's eyes as she stared at Shandra. A tear slid down her cheek.

Shandra startled awake at the sound of a roaring engine and gravel grinding under tires. She wiped at the wetness on her cheeks and realized the dogs were barking.

Andy thumped down the stairs as she crossed to the window. The clock on the nightstand read two a.m.

Uncle Martin's deep voice calmed the dogs. She pressed her face against the screen to see down in the yard and the road. A dust cloud hung over the road.

Andy held something in his hands. Aunt Jo started crying.

Seeing her family distraught tugged at her heart. Grabbing her robe, Shandra headed barefoot down the stairs. In the kitchen, Martin lowered Jo into a chair. Andy was at the sink filling the coffee pot.

"What happened?" she asked, stopping in the doorway.

"Someone left this note tied to a dead chicken." Martin slid a piece of paper across the table.

Coop will hang.

"Why would someone do this? He's in jail. They can't expect to do something…" Did they have vigilante groups on the reservation who took the law into their own hands?

"It has to be a Randal who done this," Andy said, sitting down beside his mother. "Don't worry. They can't prove Coop killed Arthur because he didn't do it."

Shandra agreed, but was worried for Coop. "We have to prove who did this so your family isn't hassled by the Randals." She walked over to the phone on the wall.

"What are you doing?" Jo stood, her hand outstretched.

"I'm reporting this to the police." The police had to know this was happening.

"Don't. It will only stir up more bad feelings." Aunt Jo turned to her husband. "Martin. Tell her not to call."

He shook his head. "Jo. We're not going to be pushed around by Oliver Randal. Coop is innocent. We don't deserve to be threatened." He nodded to Shandra. "Make the call."

Jo's head vibrated back and forth as if she were saying no on the inside, but Shandra had to think about more than just Jo's feelings. This was an attack on her family.

She started to dial 9-1-1 and replaced the receiver.

"Make the call," Martin said, moving toward the phone.

"I will. I'm going to call Liz first. We should get more attention from the police if she requests the investigation. After all, it has to do with her case." She took the stairs two at a time and dug Liz's card out of her purse. On the back was her home phone number.

Back in the kitchen, she picked up the phone and dialed. Andy was pouring coffee for his parents. "Make me a cup of tea, please," she said, listening to the ring.

"Hello," answered Liz's scratchy voice.

"Sorry to bother you. This is Shandra. Someone just left a dead chicken with a note attached in Aunt Jo and Uncle Martin's yard." She didn't think now was the time for small talk.

"Hold on."

She heard a light click and a drawer being opened.

"Okay, it's two-twenty. What time did this happen?"

"About twenty minutes ago. The car racing off and dogs barking woke me and everyone else." Shandra hid a yawn behind her hand.

"Did you call the tribal police?"

"I figured we'd get more attention if you requested

it." She wondered now if she should have called the police first.

"When we hang up, you call and report it. I'll also contact the chief of police." A pencil scratched across paper. "What did the note say?"

"Coop will hang." A shiver slithered down her back. Was her cousin safe in jail? Could something happen to him there?

"That is a definite threat to Coop. I'm going to call and have him kept away from everyone else at the jail. A Randal could get locked up for drunk and disorderly and do him harm."

Her gaze shot to Aunt Jo. There was no way she'd mention this to her. She was already a wreck.

"Velma and I talked to a lot of people yesterday. Do you think one of them said something to the Randals?" She'd never forgive herself if her questions caused Coop's death.

"I'm sure someone talked to them. Come in first thing in the morning and tell me what you know." The sound of a stifled yawn came through the line. "You call the police, I'll call the chief. And tell Jo and Martin not to worry."

"I will. Thanks." Shandra hung up the phone. "Liz says don't worry. She's calling the chief, and I'm to call the tribal police."

Martin gave her a half smile, and Aunt Jo just nodded her head.

"Too bad that officer who was sitting at the end of our road isn't there anymore," Andy said.

"Yes, it is." Shandra dialed the emergency number

and was promised an officer would respond. "How long do you think it will take one to arrive?" she asked.

"According to our records the closest one is forty-five minutes away."

Shandra groaned and pleasantly said, "Thank you." She replaced the phone and turned to the three anxious people. "They are sending someone, but they are forty-five minutes away." One glance at her aunt and she knew what had to be done.

"Aunt Jo, go to bed. Martin, Andy, and I can deal with this. We'll need you up and perky in the morning to keep us going."

Martin pulled Jo's chair back. Shandra put an arm around her shoulders, walking her to the bedroom downstairs that she shared with her husband. After reassuring Jo Liz would make sure Coop was watched and no one could harm him, her aunt finally relaxed into her pillows and closed her eyes.

Shandra tiptoed out of the room and joined the men in the kitchen. The note sat face up on the table. "Martin are you the only one who touched this?" she asked, wondering if they should put it in something.

"Yes. I put the chicken in the back of the truck so the dogs wouldn't drag it off." He stared at the note. "Why would someone do this?"

She patted his shoulder. "There was one word I heard all day yesterday when people talked about Arthur—bully. I think he got that from his grandfather. This is the type of thing a bully would do. They like to make others feel scared. Makes them feel tough." She glanced at Andy. "Don't worry. Liz will keep Coop safe, and we'll find out who really killed Arthur."

Her dream came back to her. "Is there anyone else who has a feud with the Randals?"

Martin snorted. "I think nearly every family that isn't related to them has had trouble with them."

"Anyone recently?" There had to be someone else at the lake who wanted revenge on the Randals or even just Arthur.

Andy stared at her. "Well, after Saturday night there would be Sandy. And you know about Nelly."

Martin nodded. "Last year a woman lost her job and her husband. The Randal family spread lies about her because she had caught one of them stealing where she worked."

Shandra couldn't believe the family had the power to get someone fired when they were in the wrong. "Do you know her name?"

"Robin Black."

Andy sat up straight. "That's Lyle's sister."

Shandra stared at him. "The sister at the house where we talked to Lyle tonight?"

"Yeah. I wondered where she and her husband were." Andy raised the coffee mug to his lips.

"She doesn't have a husband," Martin said. "He left her. Last I heard she was going back to school."

"That means Lyle is staying at her house alone." Shandra didn't like where her thoughts were going. Would Coop's best friend let him go to prison for a murder he didn't commit?

The dogs started barking. She glanced at the clock. It was too soon for the police to have arrived. She hoped it wasn't another threat being delivered.

Martin moved to the door. He stepped out, letting the door shut behind him.

"Do you think we need to go out, too?" she asked Andy.

"No. It wouldn't make sense for them to return tonight." As he rose to grab the coffee pot, the door opened.

Velma's husband and two other men she didn't know followed Martin into the house.

"We heard you've had trouble," Velma's husband said. The two with him nodded. "We'll take turns watching the house. Between us and the boys, there won't be a time when someone isn't watching."

Martin shook all three men's hands. "Thank you. If we can prove it is the Randal family threatening us and Coop, it will be good."

Shandra stared at the men. How had they known what had happened?

Velma's husband looked at her. "Velma said to tell you she will meet you at Liz Piney's office tomorrow."

And that was how they knew. Velma.

The dogs started barking again.

"That has to be the police," Shandra said, walking to the door. The men picked up mugs from the shelf above the coffee pot and started helping themselves to the brew.

She opened the door, expecting to see a police car. What she found was a dark SUV. Over her shoulder she asked, "Do your police drive—" The words fell away when Agent Weatherly stepped out of the vehicle.

Chapter Thirteen

Shandra wasn't prepared to deal with the FBI agent. "What are you doing here?" she asked, pulling her robe tighter around her body. She hadn't even thought about making sure she was covered in front of the men who had arrived. But the way the agent always scanned her from her head to her toes, she wanted to be as covered as she could get.

"I received a call stating Coop Elwood's family had received a threat." He stopped close enough she had to tip her chin up to look into his face. "Didn't know this was a pajama party." His grin didn't cover the fact he wasn't joking.

"There, in the back of that truck is the chicken the note was tied to." She pointed to Uncle Martin's truck.

"A chicken?" He shook his head and walked over to the truck. With two fingers, he picked the dead bird up by a foot and carried it to the back of his SUV. A back door opened and they both disappeared.

Andy joined her on the porch. "Who's that?"

"FBI Agent Weatherly."

The man stepped back, closed the door, and strode toward them. He held out his hand to Andy. "FBI Agent Frank Weatherly. And you are?"

"Andy Elwood. Coop's brother." Andy shook hands. "What have you found out so far about who really killed Arthur?"

Agent Weatherly glared at Andy then at her. "We have a witness who places your brother with the victim."

"A biased and unreliable witness," Shandra said.

The man blew out a disgusted sound. "I'm not here to debate who killed Arthur Randal.
I'm here about a threat."

Shandra stepped aside and waved the man into the house. Two steps in, he stopped. She was pretty sure he wasn't getting friendly looks from the men in the kitchen.

"Men, I'm here about the threat," he said, easing into the room.

Andy nudged her and grinned, his eyes said watch.

She followed the agent into the kitchen which was never a large room and felt like a closet with so many people filling the space.

A glance at the stony faces of the men sent a giggle bubbling in her throat. Agent Weatherly would get nowhere questioning these men.

As if he realized this, he turned to her. "Miss Higheagle, what can you tell me about this threat?"

A poke in her back from Andy made her glance over her shoulder. His head turned ever so slightly. He didn't want her talking to the agent. She didn't understand, but scanning the faces of the men, she understood that if she kept silent she would gain more of their trust. To help Coop she needed the trust of the people on the reservation, not the FBI agent.

She walked by the agent and picked up her tea cup from the table. "I think we should wait for the tribal police to arrive." The nod of approval from her uncle and the thumbs up Andy gave her from behind the agent started a warm glow in her chest. It would take time, but she would gain her whole family's trust, not just Aunt Jo's family.

"I could get this to the lab quicker if you talk to me now." The agent's frustration came out in his cranky remark.

Uncle Martin grabbed another mug from the shelf. "Sit. No one will talk to you until a tribal officer is here." He poured coffee into the cup and placed it on the table.

Agent Weatherly scanned the faces and sat at the table.

Andy moved next to Shandra. "Good job, cuz," he whispered and went to the stove to refill his cup.

Everyone stared at one another, sipping coffee and averting their gaze from the agent. Ten minutes later the dogs barked, hailing the arrival of, she hoped, the police.

Martin moved to the door. He held it open and another man entered the room.

The police officer was large. Not overweight but tall, broad-shouldered, and a big round head with a smile that covered all of his lower face. He reminded her of a big blue wall as he approached. His right hand left the duty belt, reaching out toward her.

"Welcome to the reservation. I'm officer Logan Rider."

Shandra smiled back at the man. His wide grin was infectious. If not for his size, no one would take him seriously. Her hand was swallowed by his as she shook.

"Pleased to meet you. I'm Shandra Higheagle."

His grin grew. "I know. Word gets around here." He released her hand and turned his attention on Martin and the others. "What happened?"

All the men glanced at Agent Weatherly.

Officer Rider followed their gazes. "Agent Weatherly, I saw your vehicle when I pulled up. Have you taken down the information?"

She heard the jesting in the officer's voice.

"You know damn well these men wouldn't talk to me without you here." The agent kicked a chair away from the table. "Have a seat and get the details."

Logan shook his head. "This is why people like you can't get answers." He smiled at Andy. "I'll take a cup of coffee. My shift doesn't end for several more hours." Adjusting his duty belt, the officer sat in the chair Agent Weatherly had kicked. He nodded to the seat across from him.

Uncle Martin sat.

"This has to be tough on Jo. How is she doing?" Logan asked her uncle.

"Shandra got her to sleep. Jo is a strong woman, but when it comes to the boys…"

All the men behind him murmured.

Shandra took the last seat at the table and put her hand on her uncle's arm. She'd witnessed the love between her aunt and uncle. When one hurt, they both hurt.

"Can we get on with this?" Agent Weatherly asked.

All the men and Shandra glared at him. She'd been around her family enough to have learned the way of conversation wasn't as direct as in the world she grew up in.

Logan ignored the agent. "My grandmother still misses Minnie. We could all use her calmness and clever thinking right now."

Shandra studied the man. His grandmother and her grandmother had been friends. She made a mental note to visit this woman on her next trip. She wanted to know more about the woman who visited her dreams.

"Yes. Jo misses her mother very much." Martin pushed the upside down paper still resting on the table across to Logan. "This was tied to a dead chicken and thrown in our yard."

The officer didn't touch it. He pulled out a pen, flipped over the paper, and studied the writing.

Agent Weatherly snapped on a rubber glove and picked the note up. "Did you touch it?"

Martin stared at the agent as if he were not all there. "No. It floated onto the table on its own. Ays."

The others in the room laughed.

Weatherly glared. "Anyone beside you touch it?"

"Only the chicken in the back of my truck." Martin didn't spare the agent a glance.

"Agent Weatherly put the chicken in his SUV," Shandra said.

Logan nodded. "The FBI will have faster forensics. Did you see anyone?"

Martin repeated the events after hearing the dogs bark earlier. Shandra wondered at the boldness of the person who drove in, flung the chicken, and raced off.

"We believe it was a Randal who did this." She was prepared for a comment from Agent Weatherly, but he only nodded his head.

Officer Rider finished his coffee and stood. "Tell your family to keep distance from the Randals until we've found the person responsible for Arthur's death."

"What do you mean find the person? He's in jail." Agent Weatherly stood, too, holding a small clear bag with the note inside.

The tribal officer shook his head. "If you'd lived on this reservation, you'd know nothing could provoke Coop Elwood enough to make him kill another person." He held his hand out to Martin and shook. Then he moved about the room shaking each man's hand. He stopped beside her chair. The infectious smile was back. "I'm happy to meet you. Wish you were visiting under different circumstances."

She tipped her head back and smiled up at the man. "Me, too."

Andy headed out the door ahead of Logan.

Agent Weatherly glanced about the room, a frown furrowing his brow. "Keep an eye out for more trouble."

The men all nodded.

Weatherly shook his head and left.

Everyone started talking at once. Shandra set her cup in the sink and headed upstairs. There was still an hour or two of darkness and she intended to sleep. Let the men figure out the sentry schedule.

~*~

Shandra woke with a feeling she wasn't looking at things the right way. She'd had another dream in the two hours she'd slept. One that didn't make sense. A chicken danced. A girl she assumed was Sandy, since she'd yet to meet her, lay in a dirt hole. Cold and dead. And Officer Logan Rider's round face and smile faded in and out like the Cheshire cat in *Alice in Wonderland*.

Feeling disoriented and grumpy, she dressed and wandered down the stairs.

Aunt Jo stood at the stove, cooking. When she turned, dark half-moons under her eyes made them look sunken.

Shandra shook her tiredness and crossed to her aunt. "Don't worry. We'll get to the bottom of this."

Jo's arms hugged herself. "I don't like the threat to my boy and this family." Her eyes widened and her cold hand settled on Shandra's arm. "You must be careful. Asking questions and upsetting people… they will go to the Randals and there will be more trouble."

She hugged her aunt. "I'll be fine. I have the indomitable Velma with me. No one dares to cross her." Her tone was light-hearted, but she had the same dread swirling in her stomach.

Uncle Martin entered from the back door. "There is nothing to fear. We are watched. No one will hurt anyone on this ranch."

Jo walked to her husband. "On this ranch. What about Coop? How are we sure no one will hurt him?"

"Liz said she'd contact the authorities right away." Shandra grabbed a piece of toast. "I'll get my bag and go meet with her." Without another glance at her aunt, she ran upstairs, called Velma to tell her she was on her way, and dumped her phone in her purse. In an hour, she'd find out if Liz was able to get Coop the security he needed.

Chapter Fourteen

Velma and Shandra walked into the Confederated Tribes Agency building and straight up the stairs to Liz's office. The receptionist nodded them on down the hall.

"You're early," Liz said when they stepped through her open office door.

"We promised Jo we'd make sure Coop was safe." Shandra sat in one of the chairs.

Velma hovered by the door. Studying her cousin, she was surprised to pick up on Velma being intimidated by Liz.

"I called the chief and my boss last night, well, really early this morning." The woman behind the desk grinned. "Neither one were happy to be woke up at such an hour."

"None of us were happy." Shandra studied the assistant public defender. "Will they keep Coop safe until we get him out?"

Liz leaned forward. "That's something I thought we should talk about."

She didn't like the serious tone and stony look on Liz's face. "What?"

"I know Martin and Jo have the money to post bail, but I think Coop is safer in jail until we find the real killer or until he is proven not guilty."

The woman stared straight back at her as if she hadn't just mentioned leaving their cousin locked up.

"No. Coop isn't guilty and shouldn't have to sit behind bars." Shandra couldn't imagine what it was like to be stuck in a small cell with nothing to do.

"But he would be safer. We can keep him away from everyone and the Randals can't harm him. If he's out, moving about, he'll be an easy target." Liz sat back in her chair. "Think about it. The arraignment is at one on Friday."

Shandra already knew the answer. She was putting up the bail. They'd take him straight to the ranch. Knowing her money was used to bail him out, he'd be more likely to follow directions. And she was sure the ranch would still have relatives keeping a watch for any intruders.

"Have you learned anything that can help him?" Liz asked casually.

That snagged her attention. "I thought you didn't want me poking around?"

"I don't think it's a good idea, but the chief and Agent Weatherly haven't been looking very hard for evidence that frees Coop. They think their eye witness will be enough." Liz shuffled papers. "And the fact so many saw him fighting with the victim earlier that night."

"We've talked to a number of people—"

"So I've heard," interrupted Liz.

Shandra glanced over her shoulder at Velma who nodded. Word did travel quickly here, which made her hesitant to voice her thoughts, even to Coop's defense. "I'm leaning toward Sandy—"

"The girl Coop was defending?" Liz interrupted again. "Why?"

"I have my reasons. She's off visiting an aunt when you'd think she'd be here worrying about Coop. And her car is sitting in the driveway when several people remember seeing it at the lake along with Arthur's truck. Was his truck still at the lake when they found the body?" This question had gnawed at her since yesterday.

"No. There were no vehicles parked where the party is believed to have been." Liz tapped her pen on the pad in front of her.

"Sandy went home with Coop. Her car should have been there. And where did Arthur's end up?" Shandra studied her cousin across the desk.

"Both interesting deductions." Liz leaned forward. "Don't tell anyone, but I believe you are Coop's best chance. Keep digging but be careful. The Randals are not a family to mess with."

Liz giving her the okay to keep digging lifted some of the guilt she'd been harboring at staying away from this side of her family for so long. With each trip she made to the reservation, she gained more respect and became more accepted by her family.

"We will." She faced Velma who was already shoving the office door open. Another mystery she'd delve into.

Out in the Jeep, Velma had loaned her car to a friend for the day, Shandra started the vehicle and asked, "Where would we find Nelly Bingham?"

"That who you plan to talk to first?" Her cousin questioned as if she didn't agree.

"Yes. She didn't like Arthur, and she is Steve's alibi." Shandra pulled out of the Agency parking lot. "And we need to find out how Sandy's car showed up at her house and where Arthur's truck is."

Velma snorted. "How do you plan to find out about Arthur's truck without asking a Randal?"

A big round face and infectious grin came to mind. "I have the perfect person." She parked along the side of the road and pulled her phone from her purse. She looked up the tribal police number and called.

"Hello. I'd like to leave a message for Officer Rider." She was nervous calling the station and leaving her name but she couldn't think of a better way to get the information.

"What is the message?" a female voice asked.

"Please call Shandra Higheagle." She recited her number.

"That is all you want in the message?" the woman sounded skeptical.

"Yes. I have a question I want to ask him." That was all she would divulge. Too many people shared information. She hoped just asking him to call wouldn't cause him any trouble.

"I'll give him the message." The line went silent.

"Why did you ask Logan to call you?" Velma asked, showing interest.

"He should be able to find out where Arthur's truck is and how it got there. He's a police man and should be asking questions." She shoved her phone back in her purse and followed Velma's directions to Nelly's home.

The small house in the center of Nespelem had half a dozen vehicles in various stages of disrepair on a lot the size of her back patio. No one could get them working, they were so close together.

Velma marched up to the door and knocked.

They waited as dogs barked, people shouted profanity at the dogs, and a child cried. Heavy footsteps approached the other side of the door. A wrinkled, round face peeked out between the door and the threshold.

"What do you want?" A gravelly voice asked.

Velma shoved her fisted hands on her hips. "Birdie Bingham since when have you been this unfriendly?"

The dark eyes in the wrinkled face narrowed. "Always to you." The door slammed closed and the heavy footsteps retreated.

"That woman!" Velma raised her fist to pound on the door.

"Maybe I should do this. Go wait in the Jeep." Shandra spun her cousin around, gave her a nudge toward the parked vehicle, and rapped on the door.

The same reactions happened inside the house.

However, the door didn't open.

"Go away, Velma!" shouted the same gravelly voice.

"It's not Velma. I'm Shandra Higheagle. I'd like to talk—"

The door swung open and a chubby hand grabbed her wrist, towing her into the dark interior.

"You're Minnie's granddaughter. Edward's daughter." The woman pulled her to a chair, shoved the magazines onto the floor, and gave Shandra a push that landed her on the cushions.

A puff of dust encased her. She sneezed.

"Are you catching a cold? Summer colds are the worst," the woman said, plopping down in the chair opposite Shandra.

"No. No cold." She dug in her purse for a tissue and blew her nose. "Is Nelly here?"

"How do you know Nelly? From what I've heard you haven't been on the reservation very long." The woman leaned back in her chair.

Shandra noted the house felt cool, but it was dark and smelled of fish, dirty diapers, and liniment. "I wanted to ask her about the night Arthur Randal was killed."

"You're not the police. Why do you want to ask about that?"

"I'm trying to help Liz Piney find out who really killed Arthur."

"That boy was nothing but trouble from the day his grandfather took over raising him."

A child screamed in another room.

"Do you need to go see what's wrong?" Shandra asked, using self-control to not cup her hands over her ears.

"Nelly! Nelly, shut that kid up!" The woman yelled, then smiled at her. "I heard you have your grandmother's gifts. Is that true?"

Shandra stared at the woman. What did she think she could do? What gifts did her grandmother have that this woman was interested in?

A young woman, dressed in a shirt with several holes and jeans that matched, entered the room with a child of about two on her hip. She stopped when her gaze landed on Shandra.

"Hello. Are you Nelly?" she asked, hoping to start this conversation casually.

"Yes. You're Coop and Andy's cousin aren't you?" The young woman sat on the arm of the older woman's chair.

"I am. Are you friends with my cousins?" She studied the child on Nelly's lap. They both had the same shape of eyes and ears.

"We went to school together before Fawn arrived." She ruffled the hair on the child in her lap.

"She's a pretty girl." Shandra figured Velma was out in the car hyperventilating that she wasn't in here hearing everything. "Nelly, I have some questions about the night Arthur was killed."

The young woman nodded.

"Steve Wood said he left the party with you?"

"You think Steve killed Arthur? He was pissed about how scared and hurt Sandy looked when she ran out of the bushes with Arthur on her tail." She slid her hand through the child's short hair as if the motion helped her focus.

"I understand Steve likes Sandy?" She didn't want to put ideas in Nelly's head but she wanted specific answers.

"Everyone knows he'd be all over Sandy if Coop was out of the picture."

"Then why did you leave with him? I mean knowing he liked someone else that much?"

Her lip raised on one side. Not quite a sneer but not a pleasant sight either. "I know what it's like to love someone and have them play with your heart." She kissed the top of her child's head. "When I saw him storm off to his truck, I offered to ride with him. To keep him from doing something stupid."

"Like killing Arthur?" she offered.

"No. Steve is more self-destructive. I kept him from getting rip-roaring drunk and doing something he'd regret in the morning." Sympathy swam in her brown eyes.

"What would he do that he'd regret?"

"Go to Sandy and beg her to give Coop the boot and be his girl." Her face darkened in color and her eyes sparked. "Once you beg and you're rejected, you can never forget that pain."

Shandra wondered who she was talking about. By the way she clutched the child, it had to be the father of her baby. She flicked a glance at the older woman. She had to ask the questions. "Were you with Steve all night?"

Nelly shrugged. "No. Once he passed out, I caught a ride home."

"A ride home from where?"

"The Agency. Steve's sister has a house at White Buffalo Meadows."

She didn't know where or what this was, but it placed Steve at the Agency and not far from Buffalo Lake. "What time did you catch a ride home?"

The young woman hugged the child to her. "Around three, I think. Yeah. I was home by three-thirty."

"Who gave you a ride?" She didn't think there would be that many people up at three in the morning.

Nelly glanced over at the older woman. "I started out walking. Not many people driving around at that time of night."

"I would think not." Shandra kept her gaze on the younger woman. "Who picked you up?"

"Sandy's brother, Butch. He was driving her car." She played with the child's fingers. "He said he caught a ride out to get the car for Sandy. He was pretty upset by the way Arthur treated her. He was going on about how that…" She blushed. "I'd never heard anyone called so many names."

"Did he say if he'd confronted Arthur?" This was a new suspect and one with revenge for his sister.

"He didn't act like he did. He was still really pissed." Nelly's gaze met hers. "If he'd taken out his anger, he wouldn't have been so upset still."

"Did he say who gave him the ride to the lake?" Maybe that person had taken advantage of Butch's rage.

She stared at her child's feet and shook her head. "I don't remember him mentioning anyone."

Shandra stood. "Thank you for talking to me, Nelly."

"Sure. How's Coop doing?" she asked, standing and placing the child on her hip.

"I don't know. I haven't talked to him since he turned himself in. He'll be out Friday after his arraignment." Taking hold of the door knob, Shandra had a thought. "Did you finish school?"

The young woman's face reddened. "No. Fawn came along and I went to work."

"I'm going to start up a fund for young reservation women who want to go on to college. Get your GED, and I'll make sure you get an application." She'd been trying to come up with a way to help. From what she could see of the young people she'd met so far, they all seemed to need a goal and someone who believed in them. She'd contact artists she knew and get a campaign running to provide scholarships for the young women of the Colville Reservation.

Nelly's eyes widened. "You want to help us? Why?"

"I want to give back. I may not have lived here but my family does." She meant it. Her true family had given her nothing but support from the first time she set foot back on the reservation and she wanted to help.

"That's big of you," the older woman spoke up. "Give your money but don't walk in our shoes."

She stared at the woman, unsure what was meant

by the comment. "Let me know when you are eligible." Ignoring the older woman, she handed Nelly one of her business cards and left the house.

Velma sat in the Jeep, her arms crossed over her ample breasts and annoyance narrowing her eyes and drawing her eyebrows together. "What took so long?" she asked, as Shandra slid behind the steering wheel.

"I had to get by the older woman. Is that her mother or grandmother?" She started the Jeep and backed out the drive.

"Grandmother. Nelly's mother committed suicide about ten years ago."

"Like Arthur's dad." Aunt Jo had told her about the drinking, drugs, and suicide on the reservation, but it hadn't registered how bad it was until this trip. She'd met so many young lives disrupted by the actions of their parents.

"What did you find out?" Velma uncrossed her arms and relaxed as they drove down the street.

"That we need to speak to Sandy's brother, Butch."

Chapter Fifteen

Shandra repeated all she'd learned from Nelly Bingham as Velma directed her past the new Tribal Headquarters and down the street alongside the Community Center.

"Where are we going?" she asked, glancing over at her cousin.

"You want to talk to Butch. He's roofing a house for the Public Works down this way." Velma dug into her purse and pulled out a candy bar. "Want some?" Her question was barely a whisper.

"No thanks." A growl from Shandra's stomach had her cousin staring at her.

"Did you eat this morning?"

"A slice of toast. I slept in after all the excitement last night." She spotted a house up ahead that appeared to have workmen all over the roof. "It's hot to be up there."

"People get put on a list and their needs are taken care of one at a time. Can't put off this roof just because it's hot." Velma grasped the door handle as the car rolled to a stop.

"Are you sure this is the right place to find Butch?" Shandra asked, dropping her keys in her purse.

"Yep." It was apparent Velma wasn't going to be kept from this conversation. She headed around the side of the house before Shandra had the door open. For a large woman she could move fast when she wanted to.

Shandra caught up to Velma as the older woman waved a young man in a plaid shirt with shaggy black hair to his shoulders, down from the roof.

"Butch doesn't get a break for another half hour," said a short, square man in his fifties. He took a stance at the bottom of the ladder and waved the young man back to work.

"Now see here, Arnie Deerstalker. We need to visit with him about Arthur Randal's death."

Shandra was glad she'd kept her gaze on the man on the roof. Butch visibly jolted at the mention of the death. His gaze was taking in every direction of the roof. *He's looking for a way off the roof.* Her dream flashed back. He could be the person outside the circle of Sandy's admirers who knew something.

She stepped around Velma. "Mr. Deerstalker, we only need a few minutes with him. Maybe he could take an early lunch?"

The short man tapped his hammer in his other hand as he thought.

"Please. We're here now. There's no sense we

leave and come back." She offered her best apologetic smile.

His facial features softened. "Ok. But don't keep him long." He turned to the ladder. "Butch, get down here."

The young man again had that look of someone about to flee in the opposite direction. She judged the ends of the roof not more than ten feet off the ground, but Butch must have believed he couldn't land without injuring himself. He slowly crab-walked down the roof to the ladder. Once on the ground, he glanced back and forth between them like a trapped animal.

"Butch, I'm Shandra Higheagle." She grasped his hand, not waiting for him to extend it.

As skittish as he was, she'd wanted to grab hold of him the second his feet touched the ground.

He nodded and tugged on his hand. Velma put an arm around his shoulders. She was a good six inches taller than him and fifty pounds heavier. She held him in place.

"Come on. We just have two questions for you." The larger woman led him away from the others and toward the vehicles.

"I don't know anything about Arthur's death," he blurted out when Velma turned him toward Shandra.

"We heard you retrieved your sister's car from the lake Saturday night," she said.

"Yeah. No law against that."

His belligerent tone had Velma squeezing his shoulder. "You speak nice to Shandra. She's here to help Coop."

"Who drove you out to the lake to get the car?" Shandra tried to keep her tone casual.

The young man started fidgeting with his feet. "No one."

Did he think the person who gave him a ride had killed Arthur? "That's not what we heard."

"I got a ride out to the party earlier in the night. When I saw Sandy leave and Coop follow, I knew I had a ride back home." His feet stopped fidgeting. His gaze dared her to say he lied.

"Do you have a set of keys to her car?"

He stared at her like her hair had just turned neon orange. "No."

"Then how did you drive it home if you didn't have the keys?" She had him. He would have had to get the keys from his sister at some point and someone had to have given him a ride back to the lake.

"The keys were in the car. She never takes them out."

Her gaze shot to Velma. The slight nod from her cousin side-tracked her line of thinking. "Okay. Why did you leave the lake so late?"

His eyes widened and then narrowed like an idea he didn't like had struck. "You've been talking to Nelly, haven't you?"

She didn't want to get the young woman in trouble by telling on her.

"She's the only one who knew when I drove back through the agency." He laughed. "Jokes on all of you. I wasn't coming from Buffalo Lake."

"Then where were you coming from?"

His laugh stopped abruptly. "You aren't the cops. I don't have to tell you anything."

"No, you don't. But if your sister cares for Coop as much as he cares for her, I'd think she'd want you to help prove his innocence." Shandra decided to appeal to any humanity the young man might have.

He studied her a minute. "You think he didn't kill Arthur? I saw the rage on his face when he landed those blows. Arthur deserved every punch he got. Coop really likes my sister. And he stands up for everyone, but I think this time he'd had enough of Arthur." He strode to the ladder and climbed up.

The thoughts bouncing around in her head didn't help her empty stomach any. She trudged back to the Jeep and climbed in, not saying a word until they were back on the highway. "Where to for lunch?" she asked.

"My place." Velma sat still, as if she too were thinking about his comments.

"Where could he have been coming from if not the lake?" Shandra said out loud. She wasn't going to let Butch's last words distract her from what he didn't tell her.

"People live between the agency and Buffalo Lake. There is also Rebecca Lake and McGinnis Lake out that way. He could have joined another party anywhere out there." Velma opened the car door before the Jeep came to a stop in her driveway.

"Why didn't he say that if he did?" Shandra grabbed her bag. Muffled jazz music came from within. She pulled the phone out and didn't recognize the number.

"Hello?"

"Shandra?" asked a male voice.

"Yes."

"This is Officer Rider. You asked me to call you?" The question in his voice made her feel uneasy about why she'd called him.

"Yes. The people I've talked to say Arthur's pickup was still at the lake when most of the other vehicles were gone. But Liz said there was no mention of his truck in the reports. I wondered if you could find out where it is and how it got there."

Velma stood, holding the front door open, waiting for her. She waved her to go on in.

"I'm not working that case. It's a Fed case." His tone was somber. "And you shouldn't be working it either."

"I'm trying to find the truth. According to Liz, the Chief of Police and the FBI think they have Coop because of Dorsey seeing him with Arthur. But talking to everyone, there is no way Coop could have been at the lake at the time of death. We have to find the person who killed Arthur to prove to the chief and Weatherly that Coop's innocent." She hoped her plea didn't get her in trouble with the two law enforcement officers who were ready to put her cousin away for murder.

"The chief likes things neat and tidy. Dorsey's statement makes this murder neat and tidy. As for Agent Weatherly, he doesn't want to be here and wants this over with as quick as he can."

She heard a car door close on Logan's end of the phone.

"Where are you?" he asked.

"Getting ready to have lunch at Velma's."

"Tell her to make extra. I'll make a phone call and meet you there."

She smiled as the line went silent. His willingness to help renewed her faith in reading people. She'd felt he was an ally when they first met.

One foot in the house and her phone sounded again. She glanced at the screen and smiled. Ryan.

"Hello," she said, happy to talk to a familiar person.

"What have you been up to? I've tried to call several times." He sounded more worried than irritated.

"We've had a lot of excitement." She told him about the chicken threat and her theories she was following up on.

"Those threats could be aimed at you," he said.

"They aren't. I haven't ruffled anyone, which means I haven't talked to the right person." She sat at the table where Velma was setting out what appeared to be leftovers.

"I switched days with Ron. I can be there late tonight if I leave after my shift." His voice questioned.

"That's great you can come earlier. But I'd sleep better knowing you were leaving in the morning and not after a ten hour shift." She was excited he'd be here to help her find the real killer.

"I get off at five. I could be there by ten at the latest." The words were said with determination. She knew he'd be knocking on her aunt and uncle's door at ten tonight.

The doorbell rang. Velma glared at her.

"It's Logan," Shandra told her cousin. "He's coming for lunch."

The older woman huffed out of the kitchen.

"Who's Logan?" Ryan asked.

"A tribal policeman who believes Coop wouldn't kill anyone and is willing to help us discover the truth." Elated to have someone from the police force helping her she couldn't keep the excitement from her voice.

"Is he competition?" The huskiness in his words, sent a flutter in her belly. He was jealous.

"He's a nice man who is as big as your truck."

The man she was talking about walked into the kitchen, a huge grin on his face and dressed in civilian clothes.

"See you tonight," she said and turned the phone off.

"According to Velma you didn't tell her I was coming." Logan pulled out a chair and sat.

Her cousin pulled out a chair across from her and sat, still glaring at her.

"I didn't get a chance. My friend called and I was busy talking with him."

"Tell me what you've learned so far," Officer Rider said, picking up one of the bowls of leftovers and spooning it onto his plate.

She told him all the information she had so far as they all ate. "We need to find out what happened to Arthur's truck and where Butch, Sandy's brother, was that he came from the same direction as the lake at three in the morning."

Logan leaned back in his chair and smiled at Velma. "You are still the best cook. I remember hanging out here as a kid."

The woman smiled. "You have always been a big eater."

He turned his attention to Shandra. "I have a pretty good idea where Butch was coming from. There was a delivery of drugs out at Rebecca Lake. It's west of Buffalo Lake. He's known for selling, but we've yet to actually catch him."

A thought struck her. "I never asked him about Arthur's truck!" She shoved away from the table. "I need to go back and ask him if he saw the truck, either at the lake or with someone driving it."

Logan put a hand on her arm. "Don't go talking to him alone."

She smiled and started picking up the dishes. "I won't. Velma will be with me." One glance at the woman and she knew she wouldn't talk to anyone without the woman accompanying her.

"While you do that, I'll go pay my respects to Oliver Randal and see if I can find out anything about the truck." He hugged Velma. "Thank you."

After the door closed on Logan, Shandra and her cousin cleaned up the kitchen and headed out to the Jeep. This time she wouldn't let Butch run away without answering her questions.

Chapter Sixteen

Back at the house where they'd talked to Butch before, Shandra scanned the men on the roof and packing materials around on the ground. She didn't spot the plaid shirt or shaggy black hair.

Velma marched up to the foreman, Arnie, and asked, "Where's Butch?"

The little man snarled back. "Thanks to you, he got a stomach ache and went home. We're already behind and two men short."

Shandra spun her cousin around before she said something to the foreman that would get them in even worse with the man.

"Where does he live?" she asked Velma as they both slid into their respective seats in the Jeep.

"Same place as Sandy. With their parents."

She put the Jeep in gear and headed toward Nespelem. "I think Logan was right. Butch must have

133

been stocking up on drugs and now he's worried we'll discover that's what he was doing."

Velma nodded. "Or he's the one who killed Arthur. Butch and Sandy have always been close. Had to be with the parents they have."

"What do the parents do for work?" Shandra's curiosity about the young woman who'd captured Coop's heart still hadn't been quenched.

"Father did odd jobs. He's dead. Had a car wreck about five years ago. The mother was working for the housing authority. She cleaned offices." Velma sniffed disapprovingly.

"But Sandy doesn't seem to have fallen into the cycle of her parents." She approved of a woman who persevered and bettered herself. That had been the one thing she was proud of about herself. Overcoming her step-father and Carl.

"Coop's been there all the way through high school helping her stay on track. She's smart." Velma stared at her. "Butch on the other hand. He may not be a drunk, but he's got his hands in illegal stuff. Has since he was big enough to drive."

"Do you think Coop and Sandy know about his drug business?" She didn't think Coop would let something like that go without trying to stop it. She thought about the young man's comment about Coop looking full of rage as he beat on Arthur. No one else said that. Was he setting Coop up to take the fall for something he'd committed? Perhaps to keep Coop from telling anyone about his drug business? This was the most plausible notion she'd had so far.

"I'm sure if Coop knew, he would have turned Butch in. I often thought Coop and his do-gooder attitude would end up as a policeman."

"Maybe he did find out, and Butch used his fight with Arthur to frame him before he could tell anyone." She glanced over at Velma as they turned down the street to Sandy's house.

The woman nodded. "That I could see happening." She pointed. "That's his truck."

A dusty black, Chevy truck that looked newer than Sandy's car, sat in the drive behind the compact.

Shandra parked behind the truck. She and Velma walked up to the house and knocked. Movement and talking could be heard through the door. She knocked harder.

"Coming!" shouted a young male voice.

A few seconds later, the door opened. A young man, not Butch, stood in the doorway without a shirt and his pants riding low on his hips. "We ain't buying nothing," he said and started to close the door.

Velma stepped around Shandra, wedging her body in the door opening. "We're looking for Butch. Heard he came home sick." With a shove, she sent the young man flying backwards and pushed into the house.

Shandra followed behind Velma. Once they stood in the living room, she scanned the room. The television was on low. The young man sat on the couch, glaring at them.

"I'll go check the bedrooms," Velma said, disappearing down the narrow hall. Her hips rubbed the paneling as she walked.

The young man on the couch ignored her. Shandra glanced around the room and spotted a photo of a young woman in a cap and gown. Coop stood behind her in the photo. Finally, she knew what Sandy looked like. The girl appeared embarrassed to have her photo taken. She wasn't drop dead gorgeous, but she had a pretty face and the look of innocence. Knowing what she did about this family, it would be hard for a girl her age to be as innocent as she looked in the photo.

"What the –" Butch yelled from somewhere at the back of the house.

"Get going," Velma hollered.

He barreled down the hall.

Shandra stepped in front of the door.

"Hello Butch. You didn't answer all our questions this morning." She scanned him up and down. "You're running pretty good for someone who's sick."

"That old lady scared me." He grabbed his stomach and sat on a chair, moaning.

"Quit faking. I smelled what you were doing in that room." Velma stood over him, her arm cocked to hit him in the head with her purse.

"We know you were at Rebecca Lake making a drug deal." She smiled as his face paled and he stared at her with his mouth half open. "We don't care about that. I want to know when you left Buffalo Lake and if Arthur's truck was still there."

He closed his mouth and thought. "Yeah. The truck was there. I left about one. There wasn't any other vehicles there."

"No other vehicles. Did anyone come to the party

with Arthur?" That had to explain how the truck left later, but then where was that person when Butch left?

"I don't know. I got there after he was already there." The young man stood. "You going to tell what I was doing out there?"

"No. Did you happen to see anyone on the road from the lake to the agency when you came back after your deal?"

He shook his head. "The road was empty. I didn't see another car."

"Thank you." She motioned for Velma to follow and exited the house.

"He wasn't very helpful," her cousin said, walking to the Jeep.

"We know someone had to have driven off in Arthur's truck. I would guess it was our killer or the person who arrived at the party with him." She started the vehicle. "I'll drop you off and head to the ranch. I need to see if Andy saw Arthur arrive."

~*~

At the ranch Shandra found Aunt Jo baking. It was close to ninety outside and she had the kitchen just as hot. Cookies, cupcakes, and brownies were stacked on the kitchen table.

"Is there a bake sale going on?" she asked, crossing to the refrigerator and putting ice in a glass of water.

"I thought the men watching our house would like to have treats." Jo brushed at a strand of hair clinging to her sweaty brow.

"I think they would have preferred a cold drink." She drank half the glass and set it down. "Where's

Andy?"

Jo stared at her. "What have you found out?"

"Nothing. Well, nothing I can positively say will help Coop." She didn't like the way her aunt's eyes glistened and her lip quivered. "I'm getting closer to finding the truth. It takes time. Talking to people and then having to talk to them again to ask a question I didn't know to ask until someone else says something. Now I know why Ryan says it takes so long to solve crimes." She'd questioned people before to gather information that helped solve murders, but she usually had Ryan and his job to help. This time she was the sole person searching for the information. It was hard and discouraging, but she didn't want her aunt to know that.

"Have a cookie. Or a brownie." Her aunt swept her hand over the goodies on the table. "Or a cupcake, though I haven't frosted them yet."

"Let me put my things away and I can help frost them." She ran upstairs, dropping her purse on the bed. She glanced up and spotted a photo of Coop and Sandy on the top shelf. Walking over, she studied the two of them. Coop looked like he had won a prize. Sandy smiled shyly. Did the young woman care as much about her cousin as he did her? Or was she hiding something darker under that innocent look?

The dogs barked, pulling her from her thoughts. She glanced out the window and spotted Andy walking from the barn to the house. She hurried back down to the kitchen to help frost cupcakes and talk with him.

Aunt Jo had the frosting mixed and waiting for her on the kitchen table. She took a seat, picked up a table knife, and swirled it in the chocolate frosting.

Andy stepped through the door. "Geez Mom, this kitchen's hotter than it is outside."

"You know me. I had to bake to take my mind off things." Jo wiped her hands on a towel hanging from her pant pocket and sat at the table, picking up another table knife.

Her cousin went straight to the cupboard, plucked a glass from a shelf, and headed to the refrigerator. He guzzled one glass of iced tea before refilling the glass and sitting at the table. He picked up a frosted cupcake and glanced her direction. "You learning anything?"

"Yes and no. Still unsure who could have killed Arthur. Do you remember if anyone rode to the lake with him?" She licked the icing off her finger that had touched an already frosted cupcake, then swiped her arm across her perspiring forehead.

Andy took a bite of the cake and chewed. He swallowed and shook his head. "I think he was at the lake when Coop and I arrived. I don't remember seeing him but I saw his truck." He shrugged. "Sorry, I can't answer your question."

"Can you remember who was already there when you arrived? I need to find out who could have driven off in Arthur's truck. Whoever it was had to be the person who killed him. There wouldn't be any other reason for them to drive off with his pickup." She swirled frosting on another cupcake and waited for Andy to access his memory of that night.

"There had to have been a dozen people there already. We were late. Sandy was there with her friend,

Clare. Coop was supposed to take them, but he'd worked late on something at the Archives."

"Why didn't Sandy wait for Coop?" This was interesting. You'd think a girl would wait for her guy to pick her up.

"Clare was pushing her to get there early before they ran out of beer." He grimaced. "I don't know why Sandy is friends with her. She's never been interested in anything but boys and beer."

"Why not take Clare's car?" She was beginning to think Sandy was a doormat.

"She doesn't have one. Wrecked after a party about a month ago." Andy finished off the cupcake and picked up a brownie.

"You'd think with as many young people as we've lost to drinking and driving accidents they would think before driving away from a party," Jo said, not looking up from the cupcake she frosted.

Andy nodded. "I think that's why Lyle was the last to leave the lake. He was probably seeing if anyone needed a ride."

Shandra paused from swirling her knife over the top of the cake in her hand. "Why would he do that? Doesn't he drink?"

"Not anymore. He witnessed Dorsey and a couple others get in a wreck that killed one of the passengers."

"Maxine Pleasant," Aunt Jo volunteered.

"Yeah, Maxine." Andy put half of the brownie down as if he'd lost his appetite. "To hear Lyle tell it, the crash was something you wouldn't easily forget. That's why he doesn't drink more than one or two beers and makes sure if someone is too drunk to drive, he gives them a ride. Coop always offers him a lift to parties and he won't take them so he has a vehicle to drive people."

"Wouldn't Lyle think it strange Arthur's truck was still at the lake?" Shandra couldn't believe no one questioned the vehicle still sitting there.

"Maybe he thought Arthur caught a ride with Dorsey or someone else." Andy picked the brownie back up and bit into it.

"Did Dorsey come in his own car?" she asked.

Her cousin raised his shoulders in a shrug. "Don't know. He was there when we arrived. I didn't notice his blazer."

Uncle Martin banged through the back door. "It's hotter than hell in here." He headed to the refrigerator and came back with a cold beer. "Get this stuff packed up. I'm taking all of you to a barbecue."

Chapter Seventeen

Shandra stood to the side of the group chatting about people and events she'd never heard about. Martin had brought them to a barbecue at his brother's house in Keller, a small community on the Sanpoil River an hour from the ranch.

On the drive, Aunt Jo had given her a brief rundown of the twelve bands living on the Colville Reservation and the four towns. Nespelem, Omak to the northwest, Inchelium to the northeast, and Keller in the south. Uncle Martin's mother was of the San Poil band. She'd added that of course over the years they had married and there was a variety of different bands at each community and they now call themselves Colville after the reservation.

She didn't expect to see or talk to anyone who would know the Randals but many of the older people at the barbecue came by, took hold of her hand, and told her they missed her grandmother. That Ella was missed by people in another town surprised and humbled her. The one summer she'd spent with her grandmother, Shandra had witnessed how the older woman was respected by everyone she talked to and who stopped by the ranch. But being here now, almost two years after her death, and still having people remember her so vividly, revealed she'd never really had a chance to meet the real woman that was her grandmother.

Andy strolled over. "You could be more hospitable." He nodded to a man with short-cropped hair highlighted by a white streak slightly off-center of the top of his head. "That's a friend of my Uncle Charlie. He's been asking me all kinds of questions about you. Whether you're single. What you do for a living."

She glared at her cousin. "What did you tell him?"

"That you have a police man for a boyfriend, you make vases, and you have grandmother's sight." He laughed. "I thought sure that would put him off. He and grandmother never got along."

Now she was interested in the man, but she continued to watch her cousin. She didn't want the man to think she wanted him to come over and talk to her. "Why didn't they get along?"

"Because he tried to take my mom from my dad before they were married. Ella saw it coming and warned mom to be wary of him."

"Why did he want your mom? Did he love her?" She glanced over at her aunt, busy talking with a woman she knew to be the wife of the brother throwing the barbecue.

"He wanted everything my dad had. Max lives with relatives and finds odd jobs, but he never works harder than getting by. I don't think he loved her. He just wanted to cause trouble for my dad." Andy gestured with the pop can in his hand. "See how my dad stays a good distance from Max. It's always like that at family gatherings."

"Your father knows he has nothing to fear from this man. Your mom would never look at another man." Shandra had witnessed the closeness of her aunt and uncle. Her mother and stepfather had been close but not intimately. They'd remained vigilant of one another because of the secrets of the past.

"My dad has come this close—" he held up his thumb and forefinger with less than a half an inch between them "—to knocking Max's teeth out after he made a smartass remark about my mom."

"Is that why you attend more Higheagle events than this side of your family?" She now saw why she felt less like an outsider at the potluck Velma threw for her when she was here investigating her father's death.

"Yes. Dad always says he feels more like a Higheagle than an Elwood." He shrugged. "Wish we'd come in two cars so I could leave."

Shandra felt the same way. Especially when Max strode their way.

"I'm out of here," Andy said.

"No, don't…"

He didn't even act as if he heard her, leaving her to

study the man standing four feet in front of her.

"Hello. I'm Max Pierce." He held out a hand that was pale and smooth, like it had never seen a day of hard work.

"Hello," she said, settling her hand in his and shaking once. When she tried to pull her hand back, he held on.

"I hear you're Jo's niece." He smiled. The left side of his lip curled slightly. The gesture didn't do anything to make her like him over what Andy had told her.

"You can release my hand." She gave a tug and her fingers slipped free.

"What did that little brat tell you about me?" His smile aliped into a frown.

She studied his features. He wasn't good looking, but he wasn't ugly. He was plain. That was the best word she could think of to describe him. The only interesting thing was the strip of white hair. Otherwise, he would have blended into any crowd and no one would have noticed him.

"He clued me in to your history with the family." She glanced over at Jo who watched them.

"I bet he did. Your grandmother is the one who ruined my chances with Jo." He glared at her as if she were Ella. "If not for her meddling, I'd be living on that ranch and have me some boys to take care of it."

She gasped at his insinuation that Uncle Martin didn't do anything on the ranch. "You wouldn't have lasted on the ranch. There is work to be done every single day. And not by the boys. Martin works from sun up till sun down. You wouldn't have done that."

"Shandra!" Andy called.

She glanced over and spotted her cousin waving for her to come and Martin gathering his wife.

"It's time for me to go." She didn't even bother with a good-bye. Some men didn't deserve that much.

In the car, Jo turned to her. "What did Max have to say to you?"

"Not much." She would never tell anyone in her family what he'd said.

"Did you ask him about seeing Butch on Saturday night?" Andy asked.

Shandra stared at him. "Why would I ask him that?"

"Digger said he heard Max was making money hauling drugs to the reservation." Andy was staring at the back of his dad's head.

"Does he have proof?" Martin asked.

"I'm not sure." Andy looked over at her like she would have the answer.

"I'll let the police know." Martin's hands tightened around the steering wheel.

Shandra stared out the window, enjoying the veil of dusk falling on the forest on either side of the road. This part of the reservation reminded her of where she grew up in Montana. Pine, fir, ash, and cottonwood trees vied for their spot of ground to push out roots and shoot to the sky.

They arrived home by nine. The kitchen had cooled down, but they all took a glass of iced tea and a plate of cookies to sit out in the yard and watch the sun finish for the day.

A jazz run could be heard out her bedroom window. "I better get that." Shandra placed her cup and plate on the ground and ran into the house and up the stairs. A message had been left from Ryan.

She swiped the appropriate places and his voice boomed through the phone.

"There was a wreck on the way. I'm running behind. Thinking I might just grab a room somewhere. Don't worry if you don't see me until morning."

Disappointment lodged in her throat. She'd been looking forward to seeing him and discussing what she'd learned so far. She text him back. *Drive safe and find a room for the night.* She didn't want to call and have him hear disappointment in her voice. It could push him to drive here when he should rest.

Back out at the yard, three faces turned her direction as she approached her chair. She noted the cookies were gone and her glass had been knocked over.

"Sorry, Jake swooped in and had the cookies gobbled up before I could stop him," Andy said, pointing to the smallest of the three dogs. He was a mix of several breeds. Long body and nose, short legs, and short slick hair.

She shook her head. "That's okay. I didn't need them. That was Ryan. He said there was a wreck and he wasn't going to make it tonight. I think I'll go to bed."

"Sleep tight. He'll be here in the morning," Aunt Jo said.

"I'm glad he's going to stop and sleep." She picked up her dishes, carried them in the house, and placed them in the sink.

Upstairs she made a list of what she still didn't know and who she should talk to, before she crawled into bed and fell asleep.

Ella walked out of a lake, water sliding off her. She raised a hand, pointing to an overturned car. Bodies lay about the ground around the vehicle. Shandra tried to run to them and help but her feet were sucked into the mud at the edge of the lake. "We have to help them, Ella," she pleaded with her grandmother. The woman shook her gray head. The words "It's too late," whispered in her mind.

Dogs barking, vehicles, and loud voices jolted Shandra from the dream.

Chapter Eighteen

Shandra pulled her robe around her tank top and shorts and hurried down the stairs. Aunt Jo stood at the stove making coffee. She glanced at the clock on the wall, it was four in the morning.

"What's going on?" she asked.

"The men watching our place caught someone driving down the road. Martin went out to see who it is." Jo tied an apron around her robe. "I'm up now, might as well make sweet rolls for breakfast."

Shandra squeezed her arm as she went past. She stood on the porch, watching two men and Uncle Martin talking to another man hidden from her view. One glance at the pickup parked behind Martin's and she knew who it was. She ran across the yard, past her uncle, and into Ryan's arms.

"You should have found a room," she said, hugging his familiar body and breathing in the scent

149

she'd missed the last week.

"I couldn't find one. Everything was full. I took a couple short naps, got out and walked around my rig several times." He nodded toward the two men watching them closely. "These two picked me up when I turned down the road. I take it this has to do with the threat?"

She smiled at the two men and led him toward the house. "Yes. We have someone watching the road around the clock to catch whoever made the threat. But the way news travels around here, there probably won't be any more nightly raids. I'm sure everyone in the area knows we have guards."

He chuckled and drew her closer, kissing the top of her head. "I'm glad you have guards."

In the kitchen, Aunt Jo smiled and walked over, giving Ryan a hug. "I knew you wouldn't let sleep get in your way."

He glanced at Shandra as if asking did her aunt also have visions.

She shrugged. "Do you want food or sleep?"

"Sleep. A few hours and I'll be good as new." He glanced toward the hallway. "You in the same room as last time?"

"Yes. Coop's room." The thought her cousin wasn't here to give her a hard time about using his room, took some enjoyment out of the moment.

Jo turned back to the stove.

"You coming?" he asked quietly.

"You'll fall asleep quicker if I stay here and help Aunt Jo." She kissed his cheek. "Sleep tight."

He grinned and headed down the hall.

She walked over to the coffee pot and poured a cup for her aunt. Handing the drink over, she said, "Now that Ryan's here, we'll get Coop out of jail and the charges against him dropped."

Her aunt faced her. "I know you will. It's just hard on a mother's heart when a child is suffering."

She hugged her aunt. They parted when Uncle Martin and the two men entered the kitchen. She recognized one of the men from the night before. "Coffee?"

They both nodded.

Martin walked to the cupboard and pulled out the covered dish of cupcakes. "I promised Christopher and Joey something for doing a good job. Even if the person was your boyfriend."

Her boyfriend. Yes, he was definitely that. Though their talk earlier on the phone proved they were moving toward something even more.

"Martin says he's a cop," Christopher, the man from the night before, said.

"Yes. He's a detective with the Weippe County Sheriff's Office in Idaho where I live." She placed the cups of coffee in front of the men.

"He going to help get Coop free?" the other man, Joey, asked.

"I'm hoping he can help me figure it out. It's hard though when the people involved aren't forthcoming with information." She started a tea kettle heating.

"You need us to talk to them?" Christopher, the older of the two, put his cup down with force.

"No, that won't help. Velma and I are doing okay."

The man laughed. "Velma scares everyone, even her husband. Ays."

Martin and the other man laughed along with him.

She grinned and shook her head. Her cousin was a force to be reckoned with. But she had a heart of gold. That was something she'd found out riding around with Velma.

A thought came to her. "You could ask around and see if anyone saw who drove Arthur's truck from the lake." She glanced around the table. "People would be more likely to talk to you than to me."

They all nodded. "We can do that," said the younger man.

"Good. Logan Rider was going to check on it today, well, yesterday, but I haven't heard from him. He was going to visit Oliver Randal and ask some questions."

"I hope he is careful. Logan may not be a Higheagle, but everyone knows his grandmother was your grandmother's best friend," Martin said, picking up his second cupcake.

Aunt Jo banged around at the counter. The noises stopped, and she turned toward the table. "Those two grew up together. They were like sisters they were so close."

"I would like to meet her when this mess with Coop is over." Shandra would make time to come back and visit Logan's grandmother. She had many questions about her grandmother who left before she could discover more about her heritage.

Jo smiled. "She would like that. I'll take you."

"Good."

The tea kettle whistled. She fixed a cup of tea and sat at the table visiting with the men. They stayed an hour and consumed the whole plate of cupcakes.

It was nearing six when Jo pulled a pan of sweet rolls out of the oven. The yeast and cinnamon scent started Shandra's stomach growling.

"Let me drizzle icing over these and you can have one." Her aunt mixed up the powdered sugar and milk and slowly poured it over the steaming rolls. She dug one out of the pan and placed it on a plate, handing the whole thing to Shandra.

She blew on a forkful before placing it on her tongue. The cinnamon sweetness tingled her tongue. "These are delicious!" she exclaimed and forked another small bite into her mouth.

Her aunt smiled. "I love to see someone enjoy what I bake."

"You know, if we tempt the people we talk to with these we might get answers."

Jo laughed. "I don't think my sweet rolls should be used as bribery."

Andy walked into the room. "I wasn't dreaming. I did smell your rolls. Mom, I love you." He hugged his mom, gave her a kiss on the cheek, and grabbed two rolls out of the pan.

"See, the only time I get a hug and kiss from him is when I make sweet rolls for breakfast. Ays." Jo laughed. This was the happiest she'd seen her aunt since arriving at the ranch. Baking did help with her sorrows.

The mention of dreaming brought back the scene that woke her earlier. "You mentioned an accident that caused Lyle to drink less and offer rides to people after parties."

Both Andy and Jo studied her.

"Yes," her aunt said, wiping her hands on the apron. She refilled her mug and sat at the table, wrapping her fingers around the cup. "What do you know about the accident?"

"Nothing. I wondered if you could fill me in." She tried to be nonchalant. The way both her cousin and aunt watched her sent chills down her back. "How well did you or Coop know the people in the accident?"

Andy set his fork down and moved to the refrigerator. He pulled out a gallon of milk, poured a glass, and sat back down. His mom watched him the whole time.

"Dorsey, Billy, Nelly, and Maxine were in the car. No one knows for sure who was driving. They all reeked of alcohol according to Lyle. He was the first there. The three who lived were thrown clear. Maxine was pinned under the car." He took a long drink of milk.

"Dorsey and Arthur were on the outs for a while after that. Not sure why. Neither of them ever said." He picked up his fork and jammed it into the roll. "These accidents happen once a month if not more. Kids my age and older think the only thing to do around here is get drunk on the weekends."

Aunt Jo reached over and patted his hand resting

on the table. "We've been lucky. Our boys go once in a while but they don't drink too much."

"We see a future." Andy stared into his mother's eyes. "You and Dad showed us there can be life outside the reservation or here if we work hard and look at the good and not the bad."

Jo's eyes glimmered with unshed tears. "We've taught you well. That's all a parent can ask for."

"You and Ella. She taught us to love our people and heritage. Work to make our world and the world around us better, happier." Andy gazed up at the ceiling. "Seeing Coop in jail must be hurting her."

"It is," Shandra said. Then shut her mouth.

"You have talked to her?" Andy set his fork down and gave her his full attention.

"No. We don't talk. She-she comes to me in dreams. The night before your mom called, Ella was crying in my dream. I knew something was wrong but I didn't know what." She picked up her tea cup. "Now I know."

Martin returned. He helped himself to the sweet rolls and discussed ranch issues with Andy.

"I'm going to go up and change," she said, feeling like an outsider, once again, as they talked about horses, breeding, and getting hay for the coming winter.

As she climbed the stairs, she thought of the families of the people who committed suicide and died in alcohol induced car crashes. The past their ancestors endured still plagued them with the deaths from drugs, alcohol, and domestic abuse.

Soft snores filtered through the partially open door

of Coop's bedroom. Ryan was still sound asleep. She crept in, gathered the clothes she needed, and headed to the bathroom for a shower and to dress. With Ryan here, they would narrow down the suspects. At least she hoped so, because there were still too many on her possible list.

Chapter Nineteen

Shandra walked out of the bathroom, clean and dressed. The sound of her phone jingling the jazz tune, *Dream a Little Dream of Me* drifted down the hall. She'd forgotten her phone was in the bedroom.

"Hello?" Ryan's sleepy voice rasped and set her jogging to the room.

"Who is this?" he asked, as she pushed through the door.

"I've got it," she said, grabbing the phone and sitting on the edge of the bed. "Hello?"

"Hey, Shandra. This is Logan. Who was that answering your phone?" The question didn't sound nosy so much as poking fun at her.

"My detective." Saying that rather than boyfriend made him sound manlier.

"Ahh, I heard you had a cop for a boyfriend. I was calling to tell you I visited with Oliver yesterday,

Paty Jager

unofficially."

"And what did you learn?" She had trouble concentrating as Ryan rubbed his hand up and down her back.

"He said Dorsey drove it to the house the next morning. He figured the police asked for it to be returned."

"Did you believe him?" She didn't trust Oliver Randal. Not after the dream where she and Ella watched someone put horses where they didn't belong.

"I think he's telling the truth about Dorsey bringing it back. But he didn't meet my eyes when he said he figured the police wanted it returned." He sipped something and said what she was thinking, "How did Dorsey get the truck?"

"That's what Velma and I will find out today." Ryan hit a knot in her back and she nearly moaned into the phone the pressure on the spot felt so good.

"Okay. Let me know if you need me to check anything else."

She pushed Ryan's hand away from her back even though his strong fingers did an excellent job of kneading the sore muscles. Her brain didn't function with is hands working their magic. "There is something. Any chance you could get me a copy of the report from when Maxine Pleasant died in a car accident?"

He coughed and sputtered. "Where did you hear about that and why do you want the report?"

"It may not be anything, but it's been brought up that Dorsey and Arthur weren't talking after that accident. I'd like to know more about it." She wouldn't have put any of it together if it hadn't been for last night's dream. But she wasn't divulging that to Logan.

"I'll see what I can do."

The phone went dead. She sat staring up at the photo of Coop and Sandy.

"What are you looking at?" Ryan asked, pulling Shandra down beside him. He'd missed her the past week and a half. He sniffed her hair. She smelled earthy like the outdoors and a yeasty scent that was new.

"The photo of Coop and Sandy. At one point I thought maybe Sandy killed Arthur. I didn't want to believe it. Coop loves her." She twisted in his arms. "I want them to have a happy ending."

He liked the way she thought. "And us? You want us to have a happy ending as well?"

She grinned. "I can't think of any other ending with you in it."

"That's what I like to hear." He kissed her with a soft welcoming kiss. They weren't young lovers. They were both in their mid-thirties and had had other relationships. Theirs wasn't a mad passionate coming together. They enjoyed each other, whether it was riding horse, cleaning the barn, or like this, just being close.

"If you want any of Aunt Jo's sweet rolls you might want to head downstairs before Andy eats all of them."

He sniffed her hair. "Is that what I smell on you?"

"Probably. She baked them while I was in the kitchen."

"Then I want some if they taste as good as you

smell." He kissed her again and shoved her off the bed.

Laughing, she picked up her purse.

"Where are you going?" He sat on the bed, slipping into his shirt and grabbing his pants from the end.

"To pick up my partner, Velma. Having her along has helped open people's mouths. If I had tried to talk to them alone, I would have been stonewalled."

He stood, pulling his pants up. "What am I supposed to do while you and Velma are cracking people?" He didn't like the idea of the two women possibly talking to the killer. The person had been desperate enough to kill once, they might try it again to keep the truth from being discovered.

"I'm sure Uncle Martin and Andy could use your help here on the ranch." She kissed his cheek. "I'm glad you came. When I get back, we need to sit down and I'll put all I've learned in front of you. Perhaps together we can discover who killed Arthur and be able to get Coop out of jail for good tomorrow, not just on bail."

"If I came with you and Velma, I'd hear what was said and could study the people." He followed her down the stairs.

"But you have two things against you. You're an outsider and you're a cop. I'm just an outsider with family ties." She turned to her aunt. "Jo, feed Ryan and send him out to help Martin. I'll be back by noon." Shandra disappeared out the door before he could tell her to be careful.

He stared at the door, wondering why he'd driven up here if all he was going to do was sit and worry about her.

"Don't worry. Velma won't let anything happen to her." Jo put a plate on the table. "Sit. Eat."

Ryan glanced at the plate then at the woman. He imagined this was what Shandra would look like in twenty years. "Thanks. How do you know Velma can protect her?" He sat, taking in the two large sweet rolls, two eggs, and a slab of ham.

"Velma is a large woman." She set a cup of steaming coffee in front of his plate. "And everyone is scared of her."

The woman filled a cup and sat across from him.

"What do you mean scared of her? Is she crazy?" He didn't like the idea of Shandra confronting a killer with a crazy woman by her side.

"No. She's very level headed. Velma is like Shandra. She has dreams. Only they aren't always from my mother. She's had these dreams since she was small. She can see things before they happen. Not everything, just certain things." Jo sipped her coffee and studied him. "Shandra said you understand her dreams better than she does."

"Sometimes." He chewed a bite of the roll. "This is really good."

"Thank you." She smiled. "Does it make you uncomfortable talking about Shandra's dreams?"

"No. They're personal to her and I don't discuss them with anyone but her." When she'd understood he wouldn't treat her dreams like a freak show, she'd opened up and told him more about them.

"Good. There should be that trust between a husband and wife."

The bite he'd swallowed stuck and he choked.

She sprang to her feet and patted him on the back. "There, there. Did I say something wrong?"

His eyes watered as he picked up his coffee and drank to force the food on down. Once he could talk, he shook his head. "No. You didn't say anything wrong. We'd discussed getting married not that long ago. Did she say something to you?" He hoped she had told her aunt that she was ready. His mom and sisters were pressuring him to actually propose not just feel Shandra out about it. But he'd come to know the woman who'd captured his heart. She wouldn't like him springing a proposal on her. He'd rather have her be the one doing the asking. Have it be her idea. She'd been two men's pawn in her life and from here on out he wanted her to have all the control.

"No. But anyone who is around the two of you can tell that there will be a marriage in your future." Jo moved to the kitchen sink.

That was his plan. He finished breakfast and headed to the barn to find Martin, hoping he had something for him to do that would take his mind off Shandra running around asking questions, possibly of a murderer.

~*~

Shandra parked the Jeep in front of the Flint residence. A blazer stood behind the four vehicles in different states of disrepair.

"That's Dorsey's car," Velma said. "He must have spent the night at home for a change."

"I can imagine living with a drunk would be hard."

She grabbed her bag and stepped out of the Jeep.

"There are a lot of young people on this reservation that are in survival mode. Dorsey has been lucky. Most who come from the type of family he does, won't get a college education. They'll be pulled into the life of an abuser and alcoholic, like their parents." Velma followed her up to the door.

She hoped for Dorsey's sake, he wasn't the one who'd killed Arthur. It would be a shame for someone to have overcome what he had to end up in jail for a senseless act. She knocked on the door.

A dog barked. The slurred words, "Shut up!" came from the other side of the door.

The door opened and Mr. Flint shut his eyes to the brightness before blinking and getting used to the light. When he was focused on them, he said, "What are you two doing back here?"

"We'd like to talk to Dorsey," Shandra said, politely.

His gaze slid from Velma to her. He grinned, showing mostly gums and three or four teeth. "He's still in bed. I'll get him." The man wobbled as he turned, then as if in afterthought, he waved his arm. "Come on in."

The place wasn't any cleaner than their first visit. She and Velma stood inside the door and waited.

"Go away. I don't want to speak to anyone," Dorsey's voice carried down the hall.

"You want me to go drag him out here?" Velma asked.

"No, give him some time to wake up. Maybe he'll

come out on his own."

They stood by the door for ten minutes.

"I don't think he's coming and Aldon forgot we're here." Velma headed toward the hall to the back of the house.

She grabbed the other woman's arm to stop her. "Should we just go in his room rather than drag him out here?"

Her cousin grinned. "Yeah, that would make him more vulnerable. I like it." She shook free of Shandra's hold and headed down the hall.

The only thing to do was follow. When she stepped through the bedroom door she was surprised to find a clean room without any clutter. The young man had definitely set his sights on not becoming his father. However, the sour yeasty smell in the room gave it the same underlying stench as the rest of the house.

"Dorsey. Dorsey, wake up!" Velma grabbed the young man by the arm and shook him.

"Go away," he moaned.

"We can't. We need answers." Shandra pulled a desk chair up to the side of his bed. "Velma, go get him some water, please."

The other woman nodded and hurried out of the bedroom.

She studied the young man. "Why did you get drunk?" He'd avoided this state for the length of his young life, why start now?

"Go away." He flung an arm in her direction.

"No. I won't let you ruin your life." She shoved on his shoulder. "Roll over and look at me." He didn't fight her, allowing her to roll him to his back.

His Adam's apple bobbed as he swallowed. His eyes remained closed. "I don't want any help from you."

Velma marched back in the room, carrying a glass of water. Without a word, she walked up to the bed, bent, put her arm under his back, and raised him up, setting the glass to his lips. "Drink," she ordered.

He sipped and swallowed until the glass was empty. She pulled him up, leaning him against the wall in a sitting position. His eyelids slowly worked their way up. "What are you doing here?"

"We have some questions." Shandra peered into his dilated eyes. "Why did you drive Arthur's truck back from the lake Saturday night?" Her guess was he wouldn't have enough faculties working yet to lie.

"He told me to. He said he had plans and wouldn't need it."

"What kind of plans? Was he meeting someone there?" No one had said anything about him meeting someone.

"I don't know. He didn't work but always had money. I figured he was supplying drugs. He could have been meeting someone like that." He rubbed a hand over his face. "Arthur didn't tell me about that stuff. He knew I wanted to get out of here. That was the only thing he did that didn't screw up our friendship."

"When did he tell you to take his truck? Before or after the fight with Coop?" She had to figure out if the person he met knew about the fight and used the incident to hide his involvement.

"I don't remember." He scrubbed his face with his hands again and stopped. "It was after the fight. I rode to the lake with him. After he assaulted Sandy and Coop beat him up, I told him what I thought of him. He laughed. Said he didn't care. It was about time someone took that snooty bitch down." His hands clenched, turning his knuckles white. "I wanted to clobber him then, but he tossed his keys to me and told me to bring the truck to his house in the morning, he was meeting someone and would ride back with them. He knew how mad I was at him."

"That's not the first time you've been mad at him. Why didn't you talk to him after the wreck that killed Maxine?"

Chapter Twenty

Shandra had never witnessed a person melt in front of her like the young man did. His whole body slumped and he dropped his head into his hands, sobbing.

"I think you asked one too many questions," Velma said, walking over and patting Dorsey on the shoulder.

Her stomach twisted watching him fall apart. She'd never brought another to tears. The sobs shook his body and squeezed her heart. Helplessness overwhelmed her. "I'm sorry. I didn't mean to…"

Velma shook her head and continued patting him. "You're going to be okay. Get the grief out. It's not good to hold it in when we lose someone we love. Why do you think our ancestors wailed? They were sending their grief upward, releasing it from their bodies."

As her cousin talked, Dorsey began to gain control and eased away from her touch.

Velma stepped back and quietly said, "Tell us

about Maxine."

He stared at the wall at the end of his bed. "She and I were boyfriend and girlfriend our last year of high school. We'd been out at Rebecca Lake partying. Arthur started bossing Maxine around like he owned her. I told him to knock it off. Later, when I wasn't looking, he caught her in the bushes, like he did Sandy, and got mean with her. She screamed. I knocked him down and told him he wasn't a friend acting like that. Then we got in Billy's car, he and Nelly in the back seat, me and Maxine in the front. I was angrier than I'd ever been. Maxine was crying. Billy and Nelly were messing around in the back seat. I took a corner too fast, and we flew off the road. Rolled, I don't know how many times. Me, Billy, and Nelly was thrown out, but Maxine..." He closed his eyes and swallowed several times. "If Lyle hadn't come along when he did, I would have ran back to the lake and killed Arthur. If he hadn't of pushed himself on Maxine, I wouldn't have been driving like I was."

"That's why you had a falling out with him back then," Shandra said, softly.

"Yeah. I should have stayed away from him. But his family had always been nice to me. Let me crash at their place when Dad was so drunk he walked around with a rifle and scared the shit out of me." He glanced her direction but didn't look at her. "His grandfather is mean to the family. Bullies them around like Arthur does everyone else. They don't try to make friends, they threaten them to do what they want." He locked gazes with hers. "I know it's wrong, but I'm glad he's dead. He would have just gone on hurting women and anyone else he could."

She agreed with him there, but no one deserved to be killed. He should have been locked up and rehabilitated. "You don't have any guesses as to who he might have been meeting?"

"No. I didn't ask. I wanted to check on Sandy."

"Did you check on Sandy?" She still didn't have anyone who'd seen the girl when the murder could have happened.

"She wasn't at Ruby's and no one answered at her house." He ran a hand through his hair, shoving it off his face. "I went to Arthur's and went to bed."

"Why Arthur's if you were mad at him?" She didn't understand the young men's friendship.

He shook his head. "It's the only place I have a bed any time I need it, besides here."

"Thank you for being honest with us." She drew in a fortifying breath and asked, "Did you really see Coop with Arthur after the fight?"

He stared at his hands, fidgeting in his lap. "No. I said that hoping to get Sandy."

"You'll need to tell the police and Liz Piney that you lied."

He grudgingly nodded.

"Did you see Arthur walking away from the party with someone?" She hoped he had. They needed something more concrete than he was meeting someone.

"He did walk away from the party after the beer was gone, but he was alone."

"Did he walk toward the dock?" Dorsey could very well have been the last person, besides the killer to have seen him alive.

"Yeah. He was headed to the little dock to the south of where we was."

"Thank you. I hope you finish school and find a good job," she said, standing to leave.

"I will if I can find a part-time job to pay for my rent and food." He slumped into the bed.

"Where are you going to school?" She had some contacts around the country.

"Spokane Community."

She could help him. "I have a friend in Spokane who owns a restaurant. He's always looking for staff." She pulled out a business card and wrote her friend's name and his restaurant's name on the back. "Give him a call or show up at the restaurant and tell him I sent you."

Dorsey eyed the card she held out and then her. "Why would you do this for me?"

"Because I believe dreams shouldn't be crushed." She motioned to Velma. "Come on. We have more people to talk to." She turned back to Dorsey. "Sober up and get back to school."

Out in the Jeep, Velma tapped her on the leg. "That was a good thing you did in there."

"He's had enough hardships. My friend will help him out. He knows about hardships as well."

"Where are we going now?"

"To visit with Logan. We need to find out if he knows what illegal activity Arthur might have been involved with."

She pulled out her phone and called the police officer. He was in the area and agreed to meet them in the trading post parking lot. After that call, she contacted Liz.

"My assistant says you have information about Coop's case." Liz got straight to the point.

"Yes. We, Velma and I, just talked to Dorsey and he says he didn't see Coop with Arthur after the fight. He's willing to tell you and the police, but you might need to send someone to get him and bring him to you. Not sure he'll remember he promised to do it."

"Why not? Did you coerce the information out of him?" The stern tone in the Assistant Public Defender's voice made her glad Dorsey had offered it up without resistance.

"No. We caught him after he'd been drinking. I asked him if he'd seen the two together. He said, no. He was just hoping to get Coop's girl out of saying he did." And Sandy still didn't have an alibi for the time of death. She made a mental note to talk to her some more.

"I'll send someone to pick him up. Without his statement of seeing Coop with Arthur, the police and FBI will have to dig deeper into this case. Good job getting him to tell the truth."

Pride welled in her chest. She'd discovered information that helped Coop. "It wasn't hard. We just caught him when he was vulnerable. He also said that Arthur had something going that made him money and Dorsey thought it was illegal. But they didn't talk about it. I'm meeting up with Officer Logan Rider to see if he might know something."

"Shandra, give your information to Logan and let this go. The officials will handle it now that it could be anyone." Liz paused. "Do you hear me? Leave it to the police."

"I have to go see Logan." She turned the phone off and felt someone watching. Turning her head, she peered into Velma's eyes. Merriment danced in their dark brown depths.

"You aren't dropping this until you have the person who killed Arthur." Her cousin faced forward and settled into the seat. "I'm with you all the way."

Grinning, she started the Jeep and headed to the Trading Post. "Good, I wouldn't want it any other way."

~*~

Ryan rode shotgun in Andy's pickup on a trip to the Trading Post for some groceries Jo wanted. He was glad the young man had asked him to ride along. He was antsy not knowing what Shandra was up to and after hearing Martin tell about the family of the murdered man practically getting up a lynch mob, he worried she would talk to the wrong person.

They pulled into the Trading Post parking lot and he immediately spotted Shandra's copper colored Jeep. It was pulled up alongside a tribal police cruiser.

"Park over there," he motioned to Andy. There were a couple of spots on the end near where Shandra and the officer sat.

The young man grinned and nodded toward the Jeep and cruiser. "That's Shandra talking to Logan." He walked toward the two vehicles.

Ryan strode alongside of him. The two drivers had pulled up with their windows even, leaving enough space for a person to walk between the rigs. That's what he did. Might as well check out the man who'd become Shandra's counterpart to him on the reservation.

Shandra spotted him and smiled. "Officer Logan Rider, here is Detective Ryan Greer."

He held his hand out to the large man in the cruiser who took up half the front seat. His body was hunched so he could look out the side window. The hand Ryan grasped was half a hand larger than his.

"Officer Rider," he said, nodding to the man.

"Detective. You here to make sure your woman stays safe?" He grinned and any adverse connotation was forgotten. The man had a wide, infectious smile.

"Yes. I appreciate any help I can get. She doesn't always listen to reason." He jumped back as Shandra took a swipe at him.

Rider laughed and sobered. "She is finding some good information. I think I can connect the victim to a drug related incident, which could shift the murder to one of his contacts rather than someone at the party at the lake."

He glanced at Shandra. "Looks like your work is done. How about taking me on a tour of the reservation?"

She shook her head. "I still need to talk to Sandy—" Her comment stopped short and she smiled. "Yes, we can do a tour of the reservation." She turned to her cousin. "Velma, do you mind sitting in the back?"

The large woman in the passenger seat glared at him but opened the door and slid into the back seat, slamming the door.

"Good to meet you, Rider." Ryan shook hands with the big man again and made his way around the hood of the Jeep to the front passenger seat, closing the door.

"Let me know what you learn," Shandra said, and pulled away from the cruiser.

"Where are we going?" he asked.

"First we're going to see Sandy Williams, the girl Coop was avenging at the party, and then we'll go to the scene of the crime." She turned the Jeep north and headed up the highway. Over her shoulder she asked. "You know where Sandy's aunt lives in Omak?"

"No, but I'll call Ruby's mom and get the address."

While Shandra's cousin was on the phone, he shifted in his seat to talk. "Why are you going to see Sandy?"

"Dorsey told us this morning he didn't really see Coop with Arthur."

"That's good. No eye witness." He was glad the case would now get properly worked.

"Yes. He also said he went to see Sandy and couldn't find her. No one seems to know where she was when Arthur was killed." Her golden eyes peered into his. In a lower voice she said, "Everything I'm digging up points to her."

"You think Coop will say he's guilty to protect her if you do discover it was Sandy?"

She nodded and returned her attention to the road.

"Got it. They're on this side of Omak, still inside the reservation," Velma said from the back seat.

"Tell me everything you've learned do far," he said, leaning back in the seat and listening to the two women tell him who they'd talked to and what they'd learned. He had to give the two credit for their diligence. But he hoped they didn't ask the wrong person, the wrong questions.

Chapter Twenty-one

Shandra pulled into the driveway of a small, two-story, older farm house.

"That's it. I've seen that car parked at Sandy's house before. It must be her aunt's." Velma held onto the back of Ryan's seat and leaned forward, staring at the house.

Shifting her attention from Velma to Ryan, she turned off the Jeep. He wasn't going to like what she was about to say. "You'll have to stay here." He started to protest, and she raised her hand. "Remember what I told you about no one talking to you because you're an outsider. I have Velma to run interference for me, and I'm a relative to the accused, which has helped a little. But if you come with us, I'm pretty sure we won't get a thing out of Sandy."

He glanced at the house and all around the outside. "It's pretty quiet. I'll sit tight, but if I hear or see anything that isn't right, I'll be by your side in a minute."

"I wouldn't have it any other way. Thank you for understanding." She grabbed her purse, squeezed Ryan's hand, and stepped out of the Jeep. Two steps up the walkway and Velma was on her heels.

"That man cares a great deal about you." Her cousin walked beside her.

"I know. He means a lot to me, too." Her heart stuttered in her chest. He'd taken time off from work to be with her. That showed how much he cared about her. He knew she needed his expertise and his strength.

She knocked on the door and listened. It was quiet inside. She knocked again.

"Coming!" the exasperated voice of a young woman yelled. Thumping, like someone bounding down stairs echoed inside the house.

A couple minutes later the door opened. It wasn't Sandy, but a younger facsimile of her.

"What do you want?" Her gaze traveled down Shandra to her fancy boots. "Wow! Those are awesome! What brand are they?"

She smiled, held a foot toward the girl, and pulled her pant leg up to allow her to see the fancy designs on the side. "They're Old Gringo. You like them? I thought they might be too much embroidery when I first bought them."

"They're perfect! I'm Lake. Come on in. Are you looking for my mom?" She backed up, allowing them in the house.

"No, we're friends of Sandy's and wanted to speak

with her." Shandra stopped when they all stood in the living room.

"She's upstairs packing." The teenager glanced upwards and moved one foot nervously.

"Is she going home?" Tomorrow was Coop's arraignment. She must have wanted to be back for that.

"I'm not sure. Ruby was coming to get her, but other than that, I don't know if she was going home or somewhere else." Lake leaned in as if to tell a secret. "She hasn't been talking much to anyone."

"Do you mind if we go up to her room?" She headed toward the enclosed stairway leading out of the living room.

"I better bring her down." The girl glanced back and forth between them. "Do you want me to tell her who you are?"

"Tell her it's Shandra."

Lake nodded and bounded up the stairs.

"What do you make of her leaving today?" Velma asked.

"I'm hoping it's so she can be at the arraignment tomorrow."

Steps, slowly descending the stairs, stopped their conversation.

Sandy appeared at the bottom, she stopped when she glanced at Velma. "What are you two doing here?"

"We have some information we thought you'd be happy to hear." Shandra motioned for her to sit. When the young woman did, she followed and Velma took a chair a bit out of the girl's line of sight.

"What? Is Coop free?" The hope glistening in her

eyes, gave Shandra the belief Sandy did care for her cousin.

"He's not free yet. He'll be out on bail tomorrow after the arraignment. Is that why you were packing? To come home?"

Her gaze landed everywhere but on Shandra. "No. I'm still unsure what I want to do."

She leaned forward, making the young woman focus on her. "Did Arthur rape you?"

"No! I would have—. No." Her dark curls bounced as she shook her head.

"Then why are you so shook up? From what Coop and others have said about you, I would have thought you were a much stronger person than I've seen so far." She'd decided to take a tough approach with the young woman. Using sympathy only made her act more pathetic.

"Th-this whole thing. It's so surreal. First being attacked, then Coop beating…I've never seen him so angry. Then Arthur found dead on the dock. Dorsey saying he saw Coop and Arthur together after Coop took me to Ruby's." Her eyes glinted with unshed tears. "I don't know what to think or feel."

"Dorsey has recanted. He didn't see Coop with Arthur. He said that hoping to get you for his girl." She studied the young woman. Her eyes widened a bit then her lashes lowered, hiding any feelings that might have been seen.

"I'm glad he came to his senses. Anyone who knows Coop, knows he couldn't kill anyone." She pushed up as if to stand.

"Stay put, I have a question for you."

Sandy remained seated. Her knuckles turned white, she gripped the chair arm so tight. Why was she so tense?

"Where did you go when you left Ruby's house after Coop dropped you off?" She held up a hand as Sandy started to sputter. "I have three people who told me you didn't stay at Ruby's. And no one saw you at your home."

Her eyes narrowed. She stared at Velma. "Did she say she saw me sneaking around the lake? Is that it? You brought her here thinking you could scare me into saying something that didn't happen did?"

"I've had no sight of you." Velma stared back at the young woman until she stopped glaring and cowered.

"Were you back at the lake? Is that where you went? To kill Arthur for humiliating you?" Shandra studied the girl.

A visible string pulled her up, snapping her spine straight and her head up. Her eyes shone bright. "I didn't kill Arthur. But I was at the lake. I caught a ride back with a friend. I wanted my car. I'd planned to go to Spokane the next day to find a job. I'd planned to move back and work full time until school started up again."

"What friend? Someone who was at the party before?" Shandra hadn't expected this turn of events.

"A guy I tutored a couple years ago. He's been dealing and said he had to meet his supplier at Rebecca Lake and could take me to Buffalo Lake." She wrapped her arms around herself. "He dropped me off, and by the time I realized there weren't any cars there, not even mine, he'd disappeared down the road."

"How did you get back home?" Shandra found her story hard to believe.

"I called my brother."

"But you said your phone was in your car when I called you the other day." Shandra jumped on the fabrication.

Sandy's face blanched. She could see the young woman scrambling to come up with an answer.

"It was in my car." Sandy twisted her fingers together. "I borrowed a friend's phone."

"What friend? The one who gave you the ride?" She wasn't believing half of what the young woman was saying.

"Yes. The friend who gave me the lift. He has several phones and told me to give his back the next time I saw him."

She thought Sandy was telling a story but wanted to learn more. "You said you called Butch."

"Yes. I figured he had to be the one to take my car. He said he did have it, he was busy, and would pick me up in an hour. So I wandered down to the lake." Her lip started trembling. "I saw someone sitting on the dock. There weren't any cars. I didn't know who it was and didn't want them to know I was there. So I sat down and kept an eye on him and waited for Butch."

"Are you hiding here because you saw who killed Arthur?" Now, she was starting to understand why the girl had fled to her aunt's using the attack as an excuse.

And possibly why she was telling such tales. But if the others were tall tales, was this also?

She nodded. "But I don't know who it was. I couldn't make him out, he was so far away. But as I sat there I heard the sound of splashing. Even splashes. I realized it was someone rowing a boat. The boat bumped the dock. Arthur, but I didn't know it was him at the time, stood up and took the rope the person handed up to him. As he bent to tie the boat the other person hit him over the head with an oar." She gulped. "I heard the sound of the oar hitting his head clear over where I sat. The boat moved away from the dock. As soon as I didn't hear the splashing any more, I ran back out to the parking lot and down the road. I sat at the main road and waited for Butch. He arrived about twenty minutes after I sat down."

There was one point that was unclear about Butch picking her up. "Your brother gave Nelly a ride back to Nespelem. She didn't say anything about you being in the car."

"He had business to do and took me home before he went back to the agency. He picked her up on his second trip." She studied her hands. "I don't know who killed him but if that person knew I saw it…"

"You have to tell the police. They can keep you safe." Shandra stood. "My friend, who is a police detective, is out in my Jeep. Would you feel safe if he came with us to take you back to the Agency? I'll come with you to the police station to give your statement." She knelt in front of the young woman. "We won't let anything happen to you."

Sandy stared at her and nodded slightly.

"Call Ruby, tell her you have a ride," Velma said, speaking up. "I'll go get your bag."

"I'll go get Ryan." Shandra pulled her phone out of her purse as she exited the house and walked toward the Jeep. Ryan was standing beside the vehicle. He walked toward her.

"Hi Liz, this is Shandra. I have someone who witnessed the murder."

Ryan started to open his mouth. She raised a hand.

"Who?" Liz asked. "And how?"

"It's Sandy Williams."

"The young woman the victim attacked?" Her voice held concern. "You sure she didn't do it if she was there?"

"I'm not one hundred percent sure. But when she told the story of how it happened, it was the first time I felt she wasn't stretching the truth. We're bringing her back to the agency. When we're ten minutes out, I'll call and you can meet us at the police station."

"What do you mean we? You and Velma? If she knows who the killer is you shouldn't be hauling her around. The killer could know she's a witness."

"She hasn't told anyone else, and she doesn't know who the killer is. She said it was too dark and he was too far away for her to see clearly, but she saw it happen. He used an oar."

Ryan turned to the house as Velma and Sandy walked out, Velma carrying a shoulder pack.

"I have to go. I'll give you a call." She ended the conversation and opened the back door of the Jeep.

"Sandy, this is Detective Ryan Greer. Ryan, Sandy Williams." The two shook hands and Sandy climbed into the Jeep.

"Want me to drive?" Ryan asked.

She could tell he wanted to be behind the wheel in case they were all wrong and someone did know Sandy had seen the killing.

"Yes." She took the passenger seat and Velma sat behind Ryan.

It was a quiet ride back to the agency. She didn't want to ask questions and have the young woman changing her mind. She could tell by the way Ryan glanced in the rearview mirror at the road behind them, and at Sandy, he had questions but refrained from asking them.

When they were ten minutes out, she called Liz again.

"We're ten out," she said.

"We have Dorsey's statement about not seeing Coop. Chief George and Agent Weatherly are not happy that you not only took away their eyewitness to Coop being with the victim but that you are now bringing in another eyewitness."

"How do they know about Sandy?" She glanced back at the girl and saw her tense.

"I had to give the chief a head's up that you were bringing her in to give a statement." Liz sighed. "Once you hand her over, it would be best if you took off."

"I can't. I promised I'd stay with her." She smiled and reached a hand back to Sandy. The young woman grasped her hand as if it were her only line to safety.

"We'll see how that goes. I see you coming now."

The line went dead as Velma directed Ryan to turn down the street next to the tribal building. They drove a couple streets over and into the parking spaces in front of the police station.

Chief George, Agent Weatherly, and an officer she didn't know, all stood in front of the station door.

Chapter Twenty-two

Ryan didn't like the way the men at the police station were meeting an eyewitness. They looked confrontational. "Let me talk to them before any of you get out." He parked and cut the engine. In one smooth motion, he handed Shandra the keys and slipped out of the vehicle.

"Afternoon," he said, walking up to the man in the highest ranking uniform. "I'm Detective Ryan Greer with the Weippe County Sheriff's Department in Idaho. I'm a friend of Miss Higheagle."

"You sticking your nose where it don't belong, too?" the chief asked, without grasping the hand Ryan had extended.

"No. I came here to give Shandra support. She's positive her cousin wouldn't kill anyone. I've witnessed her instincts to be correct on several occasions and believe he's innocent, too." He nodded to the Jeep.

"She's uncovered an eyewitness to the murder." He glanced down the line of men and caught the one that had to be a fed, studying him.

"Why didn't this person come forward on their own?" The chief started toward the Jeep.

"Because she was scared." He stepped in front of the man. "You need to tread lightly and not go at her like she committed the crime. She's a victim and she's scared." He nodded to the Jeep. "She wants Shandra with her while she tells you what she knows."

"That's not going to happen." The fed walked toward them. "You can't have a civilian in an interrogation room."

"Then I guess you won't get your eyewitness. She won't talk unless Shandra is present." He stood toe to toe with the fed. The man's eyes widened. Recognition glint in his eyes before he lowered his lids and backed up.

A car parked beside the Jeep. Instinct had him turning sideways enough to keep an eye on the men and the Jeep. A woman, with Shandra's build, stepped out of the car and went to the passenger side door. Shandra stepped out and the two started talking.

"What's she doing here," the fed grumbled.

"She's here to make sure we do right by the witness." The chief waved his arm. "Liz, bring her on along."

Ryan hurried back to the Jeep as Sandy stepped out and was surrounded by Liz, Shandra, and Velma. He grinned. They were a three woman wall around the girl. Everyone hustled into the police station and down the hall.

At what appeared to be a conference room, the chief peeled Ryan and Velma from the group. "You two go wait out front." He glared at Shandra. "I'd prefer you weren't in here either."

Shandra held Sandy's hands. "Would you be alright talking to the police alone with Liz here?"

The girl shook her head.

"Guess you aren't getting rid of me," Shandra said.

Ryan winked at her and escorted Velma back down the hall to a small waiting area.

"What do you think they'll do with her?" Velma asked.

"She didn't commit the crime. They can't do anything but let her go once she's made her statement." He glanced at the stained coffee pot sitting on a small table with paper cups. The pot and the blackness of the coffee didn't entice him to have a cup, even though he'd like something to do to keep his mind off of what was going on in the room.

"She's going to be a target for whoever did kill Arthur." The woman leaned back in the chair. "We're going to have to protect her."

He glanced sideways at the woman. "Why do we need to protect her? She has family doesn't she?"

"Not much. If she's Coop's girl, then we Higheagles need to keep her safe." Velma nodded. "We'll take her to the ranch. It's already being watched."

"You sure you shouldn't speak to Martin and Jo about that first." He had a big busy-body family, but he'd sure as heck tell his parents if he was bringing a threat to their farm.

She pulled out a cell phone and turned it on.

He shook his head. "Why do you have a phone if you don't keep it on?"

"I can't afford the phone if everyone calls and talks. I only use it for emergencies." She glared at him and walked outside the building.

With no one to talk to, he wandered over to a board with wanted posters. They didn't update the board very often, he noticed a flyer for a man that had been abducted in Idaho six months ago.

Footsteps echoed in the hallway, growing louder as they approached. He glanced up and discovered the fed walking toward him.

"I'm Agent Frank Weatherly," the man said, extending his hand.

"Detective Ryan Greer." He clasped the man's hand and released. "They about finished in there?"

"Just wrapping things up. You look familiar. Did we work a case together?" The man continued to study him as he had outside.

"I don't remember you or your name. You must have me mistaken for someone else." Noise behind the man had Ryan stepping away and heading to the hall. The name Weatherly tumbled around in the back of his mind.

"If you think of anything else that will help us find the killer, let me know," the chief said, leading the three women to the waiting area.

Shandra was happy to see Ryan waiting for them.

She didn't know what to make of Sandy actually seeing the murder happen, but yet unable to give a description of the killer. There were lots of questions she had for both Sandy and Ryan.

Velma entered the station door. "I just spoke to Jo, and we're to bring Sandy out there."

"Why?" Sandy asked, digging in her heels.

"Because you can't go home. You know how word gets around. The killer might think you know something and try…" Velma's words drifted off.

The young woman turned to Liz. "Do you think the killer will try to get me?"

"If word is spread you don't know who he is, you should be safe." Liz patted Sandy's arm.

"But what if the killer only hears I saw him?" Her eyes widened with fright. "This was why I was going to head to Canada. I don't want to die."

"You aren't going to die." Shandra put an arm around her shoulders. "I think taking you to the Higheagle Ranch is a good idea. We happen to have a detective staying there and since the threats, we've had around the clock guards. No one could get to you. And if they do, there will be enough people to catch him before he can cause you harm."

"It does sound like the perfect solution," Liz added. She glanced at Shandra. "I'll see you at the arraignment tomorrow?"

"Yes. I'll be there." Shandra nodded to Chief George and the FBI agent and led Sandy out to the Jeep. "We'll go by your house so you can get more clothes and any other items you need," she said, opening the Jeep door.

"Do you think the person will try to…" Sandy's hands shook as she fastened the seat belt.

"He might try, but he won't get to you. That I promise." She closed the door and slid into the front passenger seat. Ryan watched her a minute before starting the vehicle. What had she witnessed in his eyes before he'd looked away? Regret? Why? Did he think they couldn't keep Sandy safe?

"Don't worry. We won't let anything happen to you," Velma said from the back seat.

"Turn here," Shandra told Ryan. "We need to take Velma home and let Sandy get some of her things." She directed Ryan to Sandy's house first and had Velma go in with her. After what she saw in Ryan's eyes, she wanted to talk to him.

When the two were in the house, she shifted in her seat and studied the man who'd been talking to her about marriage. "Do you think taking her to the ranch is a mistake?"

"No. It is the safest place for her. If word gets out, the person is going to want to quiet her." He glanced her way. "I'm just worried your family might get hurt." He reached out. "Or you."

She grasped his hand. "We'll be fine. We Higheagles are a tough bunch. I hope the killer does come looking for Sandy. That way we can catch him and get this whole mess over with."

"Me, too." He nodded to the house. "Here they come. Your cousin is something else."

"Which one?" She grinned when he looked

perplexed. "Liz, the public defender, is also a cousin."

"That's why she resembles you." He started the Jeep as Velma set a bag on the back seat and slid in on one side and Sandy slid in on the other.

"How did your mother take the news?" she asked.

"Her mother wasn't there. Only her brother," Velma said the words as if she were thinking.

"He'll let my mom know where I am," Sandy said.

"Okay. Velma's place is on the way to the ranch." Shandra told Ryan.

He backed the Jeep out of the driveway and headed to the highway. Everyone was quiet as they pulled up to Velma's house. Her cousin opened the door and stepped out.

"Will you be at the arraignment tomorrow?" Shandra asked.

"I plan to be there." Velma gathered up her things and walked up to her door. Her long hair with streaks of gray swung back and forth like a bead curtain.

"I'm glad she's not going to the ranch," Sandy said.

"Velma is a good person. I don't understand why all of you are so scared of her." Shandra didn't believe any of the things she'd been told about Velma would make people be so frightened of the woman. It didn't make sense.

"She's big," Sandy said, as if that explained it all.

"So is Officer Rider. I haven't heard people say they are scared of him."

"He smiles and jokes. And he doesn't see things." The last sentence was whispered.

She shook her head. If everyone knew about her dreams, they'd probably be scared of her too.

Chapter Twenty-three

Aunt Jo had kicked Andy out of his room and set Sandy up in it, since Ryan and Shandra were in Coop's room. She had expected her aunt and uncle to have lots of questions, but they only asked polite questions about Sandy's family. Andy, on the other hand, appeared to be about to burst. She had a pretty good idea he would launch into questions before the meal was over.

The dogs barking and several revved engines stopped all conversation. The men all looked at one another and headed for the door.

"Who could that be?" Aunt Jo asked and started clearing the table.

"Sandy, stay put." Shandra went to the door and watched as three pickups with people stuffed in the cabs and standing in the beds pulled into the drive. Was it reinforcements?

Shouting told her different. She slipped out the

door and walked down to stand behind Uncle Martin, Andy, and Ryan.

Oliver Randal stood by the driver's side of one of the vehicles. "Get that girl out here. I want to know why she's lying to save a Higheagle!"

"She isn't lying. She's telling the truth." Ryan took a step toward Oliver.

Shandra grabbed the back of his shirt. She didn't like the lynch mob mentality that Oliver Randal seemed to create.

"The killer is in jail. Dorsey said he saw Coop with my grandson before he was killed."

The group started shouting, "Killer! Killer!"

Shandra stepped around Ryan. He grabbed her shirt this time, keeping her from walking up to the man causing trouble. "Dorsey lied. He told the attorneys and police today."

"You're all liars!" Oliver shouted.

People started crawling out of the backs of the pickups.

A gunshot rang out, stopping all movement.

"Get back in and drive away," said a voice from the side of the barn.

"Who's out there?" Oliver shouted. "Coward, show your face!"

Logan Rider, dressed in civilian clothes, stepped out from the barn, holding a rifle. Another man stepped out from the other side, also carrying a gun. Soon, there were men with rifles appearing from all directions, just like an old western.

"Go home, Oliver. Your grandson's death will be

dealt with by the law." Logan walked over and stood beside Martin. "And you're trespassing. Good night." Logan smiled.

Oliver cursed and climbed back in his truck. All three vehicles backed up and sped away, tossing gravel in the air.

"Thank you," Martin said to Logan.

"We heard a group had been riled up by Oliver and were headed this way. Good thing Grandmother's car stalled out in the middle of the road. Ays." Logan winked. "It slowed them down so we could get here over the ridge before they arrived."

Shandra hugged the big man. "Thank you. And thank your grandmother." She stepped back beside Ryan. She'd expected his arm to loop around her waist, showing she was taken. Instead, she felt him ease away slightly. Unsure what to make of his actions, she spun around and strode back to the house. Something was off between them. What had happened between this morning and now?

Jo was alone in the kitchen, cleaning up.

"Where's Sandy?" Shandra picked up dishes, carrying them to the sink.

"She said she was tired and went up to bed." Her aunt faced her. "All I know is what Velma said on the phone. Sandy actually saw someone kill Arthur and it wasn't Coop?" The anxious gleam in her eyes revealed the woman had been worried her son had killed a man.

"Yes. She went back to the lake to get her car. Only her brother had taken it when she rode away with Coop. Waiting for Butch to pick her up, she walked down to the lake and saw someone come up to the dock where Arthur sat and hit him with an oar. Then the person rowed away. She couldn't see who it was, it was too far and dark."

Aunt Jo stood a minute, processing what she'd been told. "The killer could be after Sandy once the rumor gets around that she witnessed the killing."

"Yes. That's why we brought her here. And after seeing what kind of army we have, I think whoever it is will try to get at her some way other than here. That means if you see her leave here, Ryan or I need to know immediately." She figured the killer would lure Sandy away from the ranch to take care of her. The problem would be keeping an eye on her all the time.

The men returned. Andy took a glass of milk and plate of cookies out to the barn where he was going to sleep. She'd planned on staying up with her aunt and uncle, but they both headed to bed.

Ryan stood at the back door, staring out into the gathering darkness.

She slipped her arms around his middle and leaned her head on his back. "What are you thinking about?"

He shook his head, but shifted enough to put an arm around her shoulders. "We need to keep an eye on Sandy."

"I was thinking the same thing. If she's lured away from here, she could end up like Arthur." A shudder rippled through her body.

"Don't worry. I told Andy and Martin to keep a close eye on her." He closed the door and headed to the stairs. "Come on. There's nothing we can do tonight."

On the way to their bedroom, she peeked in on Sandy. The young woman was busy typing on her phone.

"Who are you talking to?" she asked, hoping she wasn't giving out too much information.

"Ruby. Letting her know I'm okay and where I'm at." She glanced up. "That's okay, to tell her where I am?"

"Yes. If Oliver Randal knew to find you here it isn't a secret." Shandra sat on the edge of the bed. "Sandy, promise you won't go to meet anyone without telling one of us. We don't know who the killer could be and you could be lured into a trap."

Sandy closed her eyes and nodded. "I'm too scared to go anywhere."

"You will go to the arraignment with us tomorrow, won't you?" For Coop's sake she hoped the young woman went.

"Yes. As long as I don't have to say or do anything." Her eyes widened as if she'd thought of something frightening. "Will I have to testify when we do find the person who killed Arthur?"

"Yes. You won't have to point him out, you don't know what he looks like. But you'll have to repeat what you saw." She stood. "Don't worry, that is a long way off. The police have to find him first."

She walked to the room she shared with Ryan. He stood, staring out the window again. Something was on his mind besides Coop and Sandy.

While they had known each other over a year, and he knew everything about her and she thought she knew everything about him, there was a gap in his life he'd yet to share with her.

"I'm going to take a shower." She grabbed her things and went to the bathroom down the hall.

Ryan took advantage of Shandra's shower to make a call.

"Vincent," answered the familiar voice.

"It's O'Grady." Ryan used his undercover name even though the man he called was the only one who knew his real name.

"Why are you calling me?" The tone told him he had the man's attention.

"I've come across an FBI agent who says I look familiar. I don't recognize him. Could you check the files and send me the names of the FBI agents who were part of the operation?" He didn't need Weatherly going back to his office and finding information to connect him to the gang take down. No one was to ever find out that Shawn O'Grady lived.

"I'll do that right now." The phone went quiet as the door opened.

Shandra walked in, rubbing her hair with a towel.

He put his phone on vibrate and shoved it into his shirt pocket. "I have a feeling the whole courtroom will be packed tomorrow for Coop's arraignment."

"It probably will be. He has a lot of friends and family who are behind him." She pulled the towel off her head and ran a brush through the dark wavy locks.

He picked up his pack. "I'll get a shower now." He didn't miss the curious look she had on her face as he left the room.

After his shower, he checked the phone. Frank Weatherly was one of the names listed as part of the FBI sting that went down at the same time as the Chicago P.D. take down. Now he either had to come up with a good reason to not go to the arraignment and stay away from Weatherly, or he had to tell Shandra about his past and hidden identity. He took his time shaving, staring into his own eyes. He had a hard decision to make.

Let Shandra into a side of his life that could get them both killed or keep it from her and drop out of her life.

Chapter Twenty-four

Shandra couldn't stop her head from swiveling back and forth so fast her stomach had become nauseous. Ella kept pointing to Ryan. He sat on a log, looking lost and sad. Then she pointed to Sandy, heading off into a dark sinister forest. She couldn't decide whether to go to Ryan and comfort him or chase after Sandy to save her. "I can't decide!" She sat up straight, staring into the darkness. A creak to her right brought her completely out of her dream. Ryan sat in a chair, staring out into the darkness.

Now was the time to get him to tell her what was wrong. She'd deal with Sandy in the morning. She slid out of bed and walked over to the chair. Ryan grasped her hand and held on as if he thought a strong wind would whisk her away.

"I'm here. I'm awake. What is bothering you?" she asked, sitting on his lap.

His chest stopped moving as if he held his breath. Just when she was getting ready to hit him in the chest to get him breathing again, he let out a long whoosh of air.

"Agent Weatherly recognized me."

"You two worked together on something in Chicago?" she asked, even though she knew that couldn't be what had him reluctant to talk.

"No. We didn't work together." He ran his hand, that wasn't holding hers, across his face. "What I'm going to tell you could put you in danger. But damn it, the only other thing I can do is leave and never see you or my family again." His frustration vibrated his words and tightened all his muscles.

"I don't understand." Her stomach knotted as she tried to see his face, but the moonless night only revealed the dark shape of his head. Why would he have to leave?

"When I got out of the service, I went to work for the Chicago P.D. I'd only worked a week in one division and hadn't been introduced around when I was picked for a special assignment. They gave me a new identity and set me up working in a gun shop with a person known to sell guns to the gangs. I was to infiltrate a gang and work from the inside to take it down. Everything was going good, until someone got wind there was a cop in their operation. No one knew which gang or who the person was. The only person who knew me as anything other than a gang member was my captain. He'd shredded my real records at the precinct, and I only communicated with him. A huge gang war broke out with me in the middle. I was shot up pretty bad. It took me months of rehab to be able to walk and talk. My signed affidavits were used in court to bring down the man selling the guns and several of the head gang members."

"If you testified then they know who you are?" Shandra had a feeling she knew where this was going. And she didn't like it.

"An alias was used on the affidavits. They were told I was dead and a funeral was held for the person they think turned on them. Three gangs swore they would kill Shawn O'Grady if he wasn't already dead. They each lost several members from the war that was fought looking for me." He cleared his throat. "Some good young men died that night. Ones that could have helped turn things around in their neighborhoods.

"I take their vows to avenge me serious. That's why I don't hang out with my family as much as I would like. I don't want someone to someday figure out who I am and start in on them to get even." He wrapped his arms around her. "That goes for you as well. I don't want to lose you that way. But I can't walk away from my family and forget I ever met you."

"What are you going to do?" She leaned her head on his shoulder. Eighteen months ago she didn't know who he was. Now she couldn't see her life without him in it.

"I need to stay here on the ranch, away from Weatherly, so he doesn't figure it out. If word gets back to Chicago that I'm alive and living in Idaho, there's no telling how many will come looking for me." He burrowed his face between her neck and shoulder. "I don't want any more senseless killings on my conscience," he whispered.

She remained on his lap for a while before finally coaxing him back to bed. "You can stay and we'll keep Weatherly away from you."

"No one but you can know this. I don't want anyone else in danger. You I can keep close and safe."

Shandra lay awake for another hour thinking about what it must be like to know you were responsible for lost lives and you were a wanted man by people who didn't respect the law.

~*~

After lunch the next day, Shandra loaded up Aunt Jo, Uncle Martin, and Sandy into her Jeep. Andy said he'd stay and take care of the ranch and Ryan volunteered to help.

As Shandra drove up to the court building at the Indian Agency, there were more cars than a used car lot on the streets all around the building. "Liz said there usually are very few people in the courtroom during arraignments." Shandra parked the Jeep and recognized Oliver Randal's pickup.

"That's Oliver's truck. And over there are Sherman's and Moose's." Martin opened the door for Aunt Jo while Shandra waited for Sandy to step out.

"Is anyone here for Coop?" she asked, locking the doors and herding Sandy into the building behind her aunt and uncle.

Velma stepped into view, and several other people she recognized as family members stood in the narrow hall.

"What are all of you doing here?" Shandra asked as they stopped outside the courtroom.

"When Logan saw so many Randals headed this way, he called me and suggested we show a large number of family members here, but to keep it civil." She nodded to the courtroom. "They're getting ready to start."

The immediate family members entered the small room and took a seat in the row of chairs in the back. Two tables for the attorneys and the judge's raised desk with the US flag and the Confederated Tribes of Colville flag behind the desk took up the rest of the room. Chairs lined up along the wall on the right starting at a door on the far corner.

Sandy, Jo, Martin, and Shandra sat in the front row of chairs. Liz sat behind one table, a young, well-dressed young man sat behind the other.

She leaned forward and tapped Liz on the shoulder. "What are the chances of taking Coop home today?"

Her cousin smiled. "You'll see."

A door to the side of the room opened and two men dressed in orange-colored, doctor-type scrub tops and bottoms shuffled in, their ankles and wrists shackled.

Aunt Jo sucked in air at the sight of the one man about Coop's age and another older than Uncle Martin. "I hope I don't have to see Coop like that," she whispered.

Two more men and two women were ushered in. Then Coop walked through the door dressed in the clothes she'd last seen him wearing. His hands and ankles were free. He seemed surprised to see the others dressed in the orange suits and tethered.

"Why isn't he dressed in jail clothing?" Sandy asked, her gaze on Coop.

He glanced over, spotted Sandy and his whole face lit up.

"I guess we'll find out."

The bailiff asked everyone to rise and the judge entered from behind his desk.

He sat and said, "Please be seated."

Everyone sat.

"We have an interesting situation today." The judge glanced up from the paperwork on his desk and studied the prisoners. "Cooper Elwood, would you rise."

Coop stood.

"It seems the eyewitness who put you with the murder victim has recanted. The police can no longer hold you and there will be no arraignment. You are free to go." The judge restacked his papers. "Bailiff, will you escort Mr. Elwood out of this courtroom."

The bailiff escorted Coop past them. The family members parted outside the door and those inside stood, following him out of the courtroom and emptying the room.

Once they were all crammed into the narrow, short hall he asked, "Did you know they were going to do that?"

"No." She shook her head and smiled. Surely, Ryan knew that was what would happen. Why hadn't he said anything?

"Let's get Coop to Shandra's Jeep," Velma said, rounding up the family members.

"Why are you all here?" Coop asked.

"Because Oliver Randal has a large group outside." Velma waved everyone to move to the outside door.

"But I've been vindicated." Coop stopped and narrowed his eyes.

"I'm afraid, you are going to be a target just like Sandy until the real killer is found." Shandra pulled her keys from her pocket.

"What do you mean like Sandy?" He put his arm around the young woman's shoulders.

To her credit, she looked up into his eyes and told him what she'd witnessed. As her story continued Coop's face became as impassive as the older men she'd tried to question in the past. What was going through his mind? That someone could be out to hurt the woman he loved or that she'd left him in jail this long when she could have cleared him.

"I'll go unlock the Jeep's doors. The rest of you bring them out." Shandra hurried to the door and was glad to see Logan keeping the Randals away from her Jeep.

She beeped the key fob and crawled behind the wheel. Her family walked to the vehicle in a cluster, keeping Sandy and Coop in the middle. When the two were in the back seat along with Jo, Martin slid into the front passenger seat and Shandra put the Jeep in reverse.

Logan walked behind her, waving the unhappy Randals out of the way. They all chanted "Killer!

Killer! Killer!"

"I didn't kill anyone," Coop said, his frustration apparent in his voice.

"We'll figure out who did, but until then you and Sandy need to stay at the ranch where we can protect you from the Randals." Shandra pulled out of the agency and headed up the highway to Nespelem.

"I shouldn't have to hide. I didn't do anything."

She knew how he felt. It wasn't that long ago she'd been suspected of killing someone. "It's for your safety. The Randals are vindictive people from what I've seen."

The rest of the ride home, Aunt Jo told Coop about all his favorite foods she was going to make. Sandy was quiet.

Shandra glanced at the young woman in the rear-view mirror. She didn't look like someone happy to see the one they loved vindicated. Sandy appeared more nervous than before.

Uncle Martin talked of the ranch and mundane things. She smiled at him and turned down the road to the ranch. Her mind was spinning trying to figure out who to talk to next.

Driving up to the ranch her heart lodged in her throat. Agent Weatherly's SUV sat behind Uncle Martin's Chevy.

She parked and tried to act normal as her heart raced and her gaze scanned the outbuildings for the man and Ryan.

"What's he doing here?" Uncle Martin asked, storming toward the house. Before he reached the back steps, the dogs came barking from the corrals. He changed direction and they all followed. Shandra right on his heels.

Coop greeted the dogs by name as they raced by.

Her heart slowed at the sight of Agent Weatherly and Joey, the young man who had been watching the house the other night when Ryan arrived.

"What are you doing here?" Uncle Martin asked. When the family ranch was involved, everyone got straight to business.

"I came to talk to Detective Greer. Thought he might have some insights." Agent Weatherly's eyes bore into her.

What did he think she knew?

"He was here when we left," Uncle Martin said, his demeanor easing back into his usual friendly manner.

"Saw him and Andy drive off about twenty minutes after all of you," Joey said.

"Come on, Coop, I think your mom has a culinary feast waiting for you in the house." Shandra wrapped her arm through Coop's and headed to the house. Over her shoulder she called, "If anyone else wants some you might want to follow." She noticed Aunt Jo had linked arms with Sandy.

Chapter Twenty-five

Ryan stood where Andy told him the party had taken place. He'd noticed a tribal police SUV parked at the edge of a dirt lot before they'd taken a left turn. He stared toward the lake, noting the worn paths between sagebrush headed to the water's edge. "Where's the dock? The one where the body was found?"

"I'm not sure which one he was found on." Andy pulled out his phone. "I'll call Logan and ask."

"Logan? The big cop?" It was the way Shandra had hugged the big man the other night that solidified his own feelings for the woman and that he didn't want to lose her. "You sure he'll tell you? He is bound by law not to divulge that information."

The young man grinned. "Logan was the first to say he didn't believe Coop killed Arthur. And he's given Shandra information."

He didn't like the big man giving Shandra so much

help. Jealousy. He'd thought he'd outgrown the emotion. As Andy talked on the phone, he wandered through the bushes and down to the edge of the water. Staring across the water, he found the dock, decorated with yellow crime scene tape. He followed the dock back to the shore and spotted a uniformed officer sitting in a lawn chair, his feet out in front of him and his hat tipped over his face.

Before retracing his steps, he studied the ground. He found footprints besides his own. They were short and narrow. Could possibly be Sandy's. Following the imprints, he stood behind her prints at the water's edge and stared at the dock. From this distance, she could see what was going on and unless the person wore unusual clothing, it would be hard to see any distinguishing marks at night.

"Logan said—"

Ryan raised his hand stopping Andy from disturbing the tracks. "Stay there. I think this is where Sandy watched from. I found footprints." He pointed out to the dock. "And that's the dock."

"Yep." The young man's eyes lit up. "Are we going out there?"

"Not yet." He made his way back to Andy and stopped. "What other docks are there on this lake? Or places a person might put a row boat in the water?"

"That way." Andy pointed to the northwest. "There's a person's place and then Reynolds Resort." He pointed the other direction. "That way there's several people's places and a nice beach."

"Any other docks? Or easy access to the lake?"

"I'm not sure." The young man shrugged.

"Let's go to the resort. Do they rent row boats?"

"Yes."

"Perfect. Come on." He led the way back to Andy's truck. In the cab, he nudged the pack that held all of his identification, including his truck registration. In case the FBI agent went snooping around the ranch while everyone was gone. He could tell the man wasn't going to be happy until he'd satisfied his curiosity over why Ryan looked familiar. The captain had offered plastic surgery to change his appearance but what would he tell his family when he'd returned? They didn't even know about the months in the hospital and the therapy he'd undergone. He'd kept them completely clear of his mission. Until now.

Andy backtracked a short distance and took a road indicated by a sign with the words "Reynolds Resort" chiseled in a piece of wood. The truck veered down to the lake. Trees offered shade to a red-colored log cabin, picnic tables, tents, and cars. Small boats, on and off trailers, were tucked alongside the bushes. Two docks stuck out into the water.

Exiting the truck, he followed Andy up the steps of the log house. Hummingbird feeders, wasp catchers, and fly zappers hung from the porch ceiling. To his right, antlers sitting atop a bear head cradled arrows. Inside, they were greeted by an elderly woman.

She glanced his direction and spoke to Andy. "What can I do for you?"

The younger man turned to him.

"Did anyone put a boat into the water Saturday

after dark?" he asked.

The woman stared at him, then spoke to Andy. "I wouldn't know. What can I do for you?"

"We'd like to rent a boat," Ryan said, understanding why Shandra said she'd get more answers from people having her cousin along.

The old woman barely glanced at him and spoke to the younger man. "With or without a motor?"

Andy glanced to him once more. The merriment sparkling in the young man's eyes revealed he found this situation funny.

"With a motor, please." Ryan pulled out his wallet to pay for the boat.

"With motor is forty dollars. But you supply the fuel." She smiled, revealing a few missing teeth.

"Do you have fuel?" he asked Andy.

Andy shook his head.

"Then I guess we'll take one without a motor."

"That will be twenty." She held out a small arthritic hand.

He placed a twenty in her palm. "Where do we find the boat?"

"Come on, I'll show you." Andy headed out the door.

"Thank you," he said to the woman. She nodded but didn't crack a smile.

Shaking his head, Ryan followed Shandra's cousin down to the dock. They walked by a smelly fish cleaning station. The resort seemed to have all the amenities a fisherman needed. Several boats sat in the grass at the edge of the lake.

"Help me hold one up and see if it has any holes." Andy grabbed the pointed end of the boat and shoved it up to stand on end. They checked for any sunlight shining through and didn't see any.

"What about oars?" He glanced around looking for the needed tool to make the boat move through water without a motor.

"There, on the ground where the boat sat."

He plucked the wooden oars from the grass and noticed a nice looking inflatable boat with a motor and oars. Too bad they didn't have fuel. That boat would have moved them about the lake a lot faster than rowing.

They carried the boat to the dock, set it in the water, and then climbed in.

Andy took the oars from him and asked, "Where to?"

"Along the shoreline all the way to the dock. If we don't see anything that looks interesting, we'll continue along the shoreline past the dock."

The young man nodded and set out about ten feet from the shoreline with nice even strokes. "What are you looking for?"

"Marks that show someone put a boat in or pulled a boat out of the water."

"Everyone puts in wherever they feel like it." Andy stopped and pulled off his T-shirt. He had a wide chest, and while not a six-pack, he was fit.

"We're looking for a spot that a vehicle could be hidden." As soon as the words came out he had a thought. "Did you notice anyone at the party who had a boat in the back of a pickup or on a trailer?"

"No. But there were several spots along the road where vehicles were parked together. There could have been more than one party happening out here on Saturday night."

"It hasn't been established if the killer knew about the fight between Coop and the victim or they were just lucky there had been a fight and the motive was put on Coop." Ryan scanned the shoreline as he talked. There had been several places that the grass and dirt appeared disturbed but not by a boat entering the water.

Less than ten minutes passed and the dock came into view. If the killer had been as powerful a rower as Andy, he could have traveled the length of the lake in no time.

"Pull up to the dock, slow and quiet," he said, keeping his eye on the sleeping officer. No sense in getting him involved if they could help it. Stepping on toes in other jurisdictions wasn't something he cared to be known for. He reached out, stopping the hull of the boat from hitting the dock.

"Move to the end. I wish I'd asked Sandy direct questions." He studied the angle and noticed the dark stain on the dock. That would be from the victim's blood.

He pulled the boat alongside the floating dock. "I'm going to get off and stand where it appears the victim was standing. You paddle up, and I'll lean over to grab the rope and tie up the boat. You simulate hitting me in the head with the oar when I bend over."

Ryan stepped out of the boat onto the small dock,

the same width as the vessel. He glanced toward the still sleeping officer and positioned himself in accordance with the stain, facing the lake. Andy maneuvered the boat to a spot in front of him, tossing the rope at the dock.

He caught the rope and bent to tie it.

The oar touched the top of his head.

"Push down as if striking me." He felt the oar force him forward, toward the boat. "If the person had struck him that way, the victim would have been half in the boat with them." He sat back on his haunches. "Let's do it again only this time, swing it like a bat to the side of my head."

He straightened and glanced at the officer again, while Andy recoiled the rope. The end flew toward him. He caught it and leaned down to fasten the boat to the dock. The oar touched his left temple. "Push it on through," he said, allowing the paddle to send him sideways along the length of the dock.

Blood splatter covered the dock under him. The larger dark spot was on the opposite side. "He was struck by a left-handed person."

"How do you know that?" Andy asked, holding onto the dock to keep the boat alongside.

"Hey! What are you doing?" The officer was on his feet and striding toward them.

Ryan ignored the man and explained his findings to Andy. "The blood spatter, what happens when a person is hit, is here." He tapped the dock before pushing to his feet. "This spot is where he landed and bled out." Ryan stared at the dark spot on the dock. "Any of the people

Shandra's been talking to left-handed?"

The young man shrugged. "I don't pay that much attention."

"This is a crime scene. You're not supposed—Hi, Andy. You know you shouldn't be here." Officer Walker, the name badge said, glared at him as he spoke to Andy.

"This is Ryan Greer, he's a detective and a friend of my cousin Shandra." Andy waved a hand toward him.

Officer Walker shifted his full attention to Ryan. "What are you doing here?"

"I just wanted to see the crime scene and get an idea of what happened."

The officer cocked his head to one side. "You think the police on the reservation don't know what they're doing?"

"No. Just professional curiosity." He climbed back into the boat. "Have any of the forensics came back from the lab?"

The man shrugged. "I'm only here to keep people away from the crime scene. You'll have to talk to the chief about that."

"Thanks, I will." He shoved the boat away from the dock.

Andy took his cue and started paddling.

"Want me to row?" Ryan asked, when they were out of earshot of the officer standing on the dock watching them.

"No, I don't mind doing it."

"Keep on around this side of the lake close to the

edge. We still don't know where the murderer put his boat in."

Chapter Twenty-six

Shandra turned from pouring lemonade in glasses and found Agent Weatherly standing at the door with Uncle Martin right behind him. She had invited everyone to the kitchen but had hoped the agent would take the hint and leave. After hearing Ryan's past and his fear of gang retaliation, she had to remain clear-headed and not let this man think she knew anything.

"Are you going to start looking for the real killer now that Coop has been released?" she asked, setting the glasses on the table while Aunt Jo placed plates of cookies and treats in the middle.

"We have been looking for the murderer." Agent Weatherly took a seat beside Coop. "We'll have more forensic evidence back on Monday." He picked up a cookie and stared at her cousin. "That bother you, knowing we'll know more next week?"

"Nope. I hope you get enough evidence to find out

who really did it. I'm tired of being called killer and being treated like one." Coop drank down half a glass of lemonade and narrowed his gaze on the agent. "What are you doing to protect Sandy? She saw it happen. Even though she didn't see who, he could be planning to hurt her."

Shandra watched the young woman freeze a moment before scooting a little closer to Coop.

"We're aware of Miss Williams's statement." The agent focused on Sandy. "Can you think of anything about the person that might help us figure out who he could be?" He bit into the cookie, watching her.

With the man focused on Sandy, Shandra slipped out of the kitchen and up to the bedroom. Pulling her phone from her pocket, she called Ryan.

"Hello. How did the arraignment go?" he asked.

"Good. Coop was released due to lack of evidence. But you knew that was going to happen didn't you?"

"I had my suspicions."

"Where are you?" It sounded like water splashing rhythmically.

"On Buffalo Lake. We're trying to figure out where the murderer put a boat in at." There was a pause. "I think the person we're looking for is left handed."

"Why do you say that?" She hadn't paid attention to which hand people favored when she interviewed them.

"Andy and I ran through the scenario at the dock. Using the blood spatter and bleed out, it appears the killer was left handed."

Her mind ran back over what he'd told her about the forensic report. "How could Arthur getting hit in the back of the head tell you if the killer was left handed?"

"Good question. I was thinking about what Sandy said and not the report. Still, watch out if you run across a lefty."

She plugged that into the other information about this case in her head. "You need to stay away a while longer."

"Why?" Suspicion coated the one word.

"Agent Weatherly is here, and he came specifically to see you. He used the ruse that you might be useful in this investigation." She thought how that sounded and added. "Which you are, but you know why he is here."

Ryan laughed. "I knew what you meant. Give me a call when he leaves. I imagine we'll be here another hour or two anyway."

"Happy hunting." She shut down the phone, shoved it in her back pocket, and returned to the kitchen.

To her surprise Weatherly was no longer at the table. "Where did the agent go?" she asked, picking up a cookie.

"Said he was headed to Buffalo Lake." Coop raised his glass and drained the remaining liquid.

Shandra pulled out her phone and text Ryan the message Weatherly was headed for the lake. Her heart raced in her chest. She didn't know what the agent would do if he put two and two together. But Ryan's fear of anyone finding out who he'd been was enough to make her paranoid.

"What's wrong?" Coop asked, waving his hand up and down in front of her face.

"Nothing. Just thinking." She shoved her worries for Ryan to the back of her mind and focused on the two young people sitting at the table. While they appeared to like one another, she'd noticed they didn't hold hands or touch.

"Do either of you know anyone who is left-handed?" She bit into the cookie in her hand and studied the two.

Sandy shook her head. Then stopped. "My uncle."

"I know several people who can do things with both hands but not consistently use their left hand. Why?" Coop stood, plucked the pitcher of lemonade from the counter, and refilled the glasses.

"Ryan thinks the killer could have been left-handed." She shifted her attention to Sandy. "Do you remember how the person struck Arthur?"

The young woman gulped. Coop's hand captured hers.

"I've been trying to forget what I saw." She closed her eyes, and they sprang open. "He swung the oar from the side."

"Which way?" Shandra swung from her right and then her left.

"That way."

It confirmed Ryan's assumption the killer was left handed. She stood. "I want you two to stay here. Don't go anywhere."

"Where are you going?" Coop asked.

"Fishing with Velma." She smiled at the two

confused faces and bounded upstairs for her purse and Jeep keys.

~*~

Ryan read the text from Shandra and groaned. The agent was most likely taking a second look at the crime scene. They were around several arms of land away from there.

"Who lives here?" he asked, as they paddled by a house with a dock jutting out into the lake. It was the first residence they'd paddled by so far.

"I'm not sure." Andy wiped at the sweat on his brow.

"Let me take over." Ryan tossed the young man a bottle of water from his pack. He made a mental note to check out who that house belonged to.

Andy dropped the oars to catch the bottle. One nearly slipped into the water before he caught it. "That was close. Rowing back with one oar would have stunk."

"I agree." They shifted spots, and Ryan picked up the oars, surging the boat through the calm water. He kept his gaze on the shoreline. So far the only paths to the water appeared to be made by wildlife. Following the arm of land sticking out into the water, he checked his watch to keep track of the time it took to get from the dock to any spot that appeared to have been used to shove a boat into the water.

He continued along, studying the shoreline.

"There's something floating over there." Andy pointed to a spot over Ryan's shoulder.

Maneuvering the boat closer to shore, sunlight glint

off a metal handle. Andy reached out to grab the handle.

"Don't!" He pulled the young man's hand back. Using his oar, he flipped the handle and revealed a wooden paddle on the end of the aluminum handle.

"Think someone lost an oar?" Andy asked.

Ryan pulled the boat closer to inspect the oar they'd found. A few strands of hair were lodged in a crack of the wooden paddle.

"We need to have the officer at the crime scene come down here and stand guard over this until someone collects it for evidence." He glanced at Shandra's cousin. "You don't happen to know his cell number do you?"

"No. You could call the police station and they could tell him to come down here or one of us could row back to get him."

He pulled his phone out of his holder and saw the text message from Shandra. He noted the time. Weatherly had to be here by now.

"You take the boat and go notify the officer. I have a suspicion the FBI agent will be there too. Don't tell him I'm here with the oar, just say you found an oar with hair stuck to it."

Andy's face lit up and he stared at the oar. "Really? Hair. Like Arthur's?"

"It could be or it could be something else." He grabbed the young man's shoulder to get his attention. "You dropped me off down farther and then saw this on your way to get the pickup." He nodded down the shoreline of the lake. "You stay until they bag this as evidence, then get your truck and go to that first house between here and the resort. I'll be around there somewhere."

The younger man studied him. "Why are you staying away from the FBI agent?"

"I'm not staying away. I'm staying out of the way. Most FBI agents don't like cops, especially those not in the jurisdiction they are working, finding clues they should have already found." He stepped out of the boat and grabbed his backpack. "See you in a couple hours."

Andy sat in the boat watching him walking along the shoreline. "Go on! Get to that dock and the officer."

Shandra's cousin finally paddled off. Ryan adjusted his backpack and headed back along the water's edge.

Chapter Twenty-seven

Shandra picked up Velma and they headed for the Ketch Pen tavern.

"Why are we going to the Ketch Pen?" Velma asked, settling her handbag on her lap.

"I want to talk to Billy Crow and see if Dorsey has stayed sober since we last talked with him."

"You still suspect one of those two?" Her cousin didn't sound convinced either of the young men could kill someone.

"I'm not ruling them out, but I think it has more to do with drugs than Sandy. I think both of them may know more about Arthur's involvement in that than they have said so far." She liked both of the young men, but while she'd grown up wearing blinders, she'd since learned that no one was above killing another person if the right emotions were triggered.

She parked alongside Billy Crow's truck and

nodded when Velma pointed to Dorsey's blazer.

"Oh look, Lyle is here, too." Velma pointed to a beat-up, older pickup.

"I would have thought he'd have a nicer vehicle than that," she said, stepping out of the Jeep and moving toward the building.

"That was his grandfather's. The two of them were close." Velma pulled the door open. Stale beer, cigarette smoke, and body odor wafted out the door.

"Is Lyle close to his sister, Robin?" She walked in, scanned the room for the young men, and was surprised to see them all sitting at a table with their heads together deep in conversation.

She nudged Velma, and they both walked over to the table.

"There's only one way to stop—" Lyle shut his mouth as Dorsey elbowed him in the side and stared at Velma.

"Hello," Shandra said, grabbing a chair from the next table and sitting down between Dorsey and Billy. "I'm surprised to see you three sitting at the same table."

"Why?" Lyle asked, his voice iced with irritation.

"You're best friends with Coop." She pointed to Dorsey. "You're best friends with Arthur and you," she pointed to Billy, "Didn't seem to care for either one of them."

All three blushed. Billy stared at the glass of beer in front of him. Dorsey drew circles in the moisture on the table in front of him, and Lyle glared at her.

She was beginning to wonder what Coop saw in his

friend Lyle.

"You do know that Coop is out of jail." Her gaze landed on each one, lingering on Lyle.

"Yeah, Dorsey said he told the police that he made that up about Coop and Arthur." Lyle slapped the other young man on the back. "It was the right thing to do."

"It was. And now I hope all of you to do the right thing and answer my questions truthfully." She scanned the three young men.

Billy picked up his glass with his right hand and took a drink. There was a glass of iced tea in front of Lyle, and Dorsey had a wet ring in front of him but no glass. He made figure eights in the water with a finger from his left hand.

"I would have thought you were out of questions by now." Lyle, again being combative. What did he have to hide? Had he killed Arthur and left his best friend to take the consequences? It didn't make sense considering he no longer drank and took care of others who did.

"I know that Dorsey drove Arthur's truck back and that Butch brought Sandy's car back."

"How is Sandy?" Dorsey asked. He nodded to the other two. "We heard she saw it happen."

"She's fine. How did you hear about Sandy?" This knowledge might help find the killer.

Billy shrugged. "I heard it from Big Bear over at the gas station."

Great, the person filling people's cars with fuel was also filling them with rumors.

"I heard it from Ruby. She called to let me know

Sandy was okay." Dorsey's face reddened.

He was still checking up on the young woman. Did she love Dorsey but knew Coop was more stable? That was a question she was going to ask the next time she saw Sandy.

She glanced at Lyle. "Where did you hear it?"

"From Coop. He called me a while ago. Glad he's out of jail." The young man did appear relieved for his friend.

Back to the question. "How would Arthur have tried to get home without a car to drive?"

Dorsey leaned back and the waitress set a bubbly clear drink in front of him. "He would have called his grandfather for a ride." He picked the glass up with his right hand and drank.

His grandfather. "Do you think he did? And would he have driven out to the lake and picked Arthur up?"

Dorsey was the most knowledgeable of the Randal family. She watched him as he thought. "I don't think he's ever picked Arthur up when he was drunk. I know there were several times Arthur would come to school late and said he'd gotten drunk and slept out all night until he could catch a ride home with someone driving down the closest road."

"There was mention he planned to meet someone. What do any of you know about his involvement with drugs on the reservation?" This was the question she knew they would balk at answering. They all three visibly shrank and avoided eye contact.

"Come on. I'm not saying any of you use the stuff, but the way rumors spread around here, there has to be talk that connects Arthur to the drugs coming in, or even a name of the person who is orchestrating the whole thing."

Billy squirmed.

"What do you know, Billy?" She waved her hand to the bartender to bring another round.

"I know that Chief George is trying to crack down on the stuff coming in." He smiled when the waitress set another beer next to the one he'd sipped down to half.

"We'll have a basket of fries and two more iced teas," she told the waitress before returning her attention to Billy. "Have you heard of any names he's interested in?"

The young man downed the last half of his beer, wiped the back of his hand across his mouth, and leaned forward. "Some guy bought a house on Buffalo Lake. They use the road from highway one-fifty-five to Rebecca Lake to bring them to the house on Buffalo Lake."

"Why hasn't the chief raided that house?" She didn't understand, if Billy knew this much surely the police did too.

"There's someone on the tribal police who tells them there's going to be a raid and they don't find anything when they get there." Billy shrugged.

Corrupt police. They seemed to be everywhere, overshadowing the millions of good ones.

"How do the drugs get onto the reservation? Do they drive right up the highway?" She hadn't seen any road blocks or patrol cars when she arrived.

"They bring them by boat up to Keller."

She perked up, remembering the oily man at the barbecue and how Andy said the rumors had Max linked to drugs.

Right now the drug route wasn't getting her any closer to who killed Arthur. Unless… "Are there any Randals on the tribal police?"

"Arthur's cousin, Barney," Dorsey offered.

"What about Butch Williams? Any of you know if he has anything to do with the drugs coming into the reservation." All three nodded.

But wouldn't Sandy recognize her own brother even from that far away?

~*~

Ryan was sweaty, hot, and thirsty by the time he reached the house closest to the resort. Trying to stay away from the FBI agent was becoming a pain. If he didn't have two sisters, a brother, mother, father, and nieces and nephews to protect, he'd just face the man, let him figure it out and take care of any gang member that came for him. But he had a large family that he knew would never be safe if his undercover identity was matched to his true identity.

He sat down in the shade of a tree near the road leading into the house and drank from his water bottle. He didn't know how long it would be before Andy came to get him. After a few more swallows of water, he pulled out his phone and scrolled through the names.

"Hello? Where are you?" Shandra asked, seconds after the first ring on his phone.

"I'm sitting under a tree waiting for Andy to pick

me up. What are you doing?" He drank more water and watched the lake.

"Why are you waiting for Andy?" The sound of someone else talking drifted through his phone.

"Avoiding Weatherly. Who are you with?" He listened closer and knew who she was going to say.

"Logan and Velma. We had an interesting chat with Billy, Dorsey, and Lyle and thought the police should know what we'd learned."

"What did you learn?" He needed something to keep his mind from jumping to conclusions about her and the large police officer. From her past, he knew Shandra was slow letting her guard down with people. But that's what made her hugging Rider the other day send up flags he needed to get her committed to him.

"There is a group who smuggle drugs onto the reservation and then distributes them. Seems they were always a step ahead of the law. There is a Randal on the tribal police."

It didn't take him long to put two and two together. "You think Arthur was killed because of the drug running?"

"It makes more sense than anything else we've found out."

A cloud of dust on the main road, coming from the resort direction, had him peering through the dust to see if it was his ride. He stepped behind the tree. "Looks like my ride is here. I'll catch up to you back at the ranch." Sliding his finger across the screen, he peered out from behind the tree.

It wasn't Andy's truck causing the dust storm. He

relaxed a little, noting it wasn't Weatherly's SUV either. But he remained hidden. If it was the property owner returning, he didn't want the person to think he was lurking or planning to rob him and call the police.

He watched a man close to his age and a younger man get out of the fancy car and walk into a single-wide mobile home, like an on-site construction office. There was a larger double-wide that looked as if it had seen better days. Both men were dressed in nice clothes, as if they'd come from a business meeting. While he hadn't encountered many people other than law enforcement and Shandra's family, he found their clothing and presence interesting.

Curiosity sent him scurrying from his tree to the bushes and up to the outside of the smaller building. He listened under an open window. The constant drone of a fan muffled the voices inside. They spoke low and there were three distinct voices. Someone had been in the trailer before the men arrived. That person could have watched him walk up the road and ask if they saw him.

He glanced back to the road and spotted a dust cloud. Someone was coming down the drive to the house. If it wasn't Andy, he could get caught spying, and if it was Andy, someone could come out of the building and catch him spying. Reluctant to leave without knowing more about the two men but not wanting to get Andy caught up in something of his doing, he hurried back to the tree.

When he recognized the truck, he stepped out of the shade and stopped Andy from continuing on to the buildings. In the cab, he swirled his finger. "Turn around here."

The young man stared at him for only a second and turned the truck around.

"Did the oar get into the police's hands?" he asked.

"Yes. Agent Weatherly asked where you were. He knew that we left the ranch together." Andy didn't look at him, just pressed on the accelerator.

"And?" He knew it was wrong to have Shandra's cousin lie to the FBI but he also knew Shandra would understand.

"He studied me a bit and then took the oar and left." He slowed to make the turn onto the main road. "I waited to make sure he was gone, then rowed back to the resort and grabbed my truck."

"Did you see him on your way here?"

"No. Why did you make me turn around before anyone at that house saw me?"

The young man had good reasoning skills. "While I waited for you..." He told Andy about the men and not being able to hear the conversation.

"What did the two look like? Maybe I might know them."

"The older man was average, thin and had a white streak in his hair."

"That sounds like Max Pierce. A friend of my uncle Charlie. Rumor is he is the one bringing the drugs into the reservation."

Knowing he'd been that close to a drug trafficker and couldn't do anything because it was out of his jurisdiction, sent his jaw twitching as he clenched his teeth. Were they setting up another delivery? Should he have snooped around to see if there were any drugs on the premise and then called the tribal police?

"What are you thinking?" Andy asked, slowing the truck.

"That I should have gathered evidence to catch those bastards."

Chapter Twenty-eight

Shandra dropped Velma off at her house and headed back to the ranch. They'd given Logan all the information they'd pulled out of the three at the Ketch Pen. How love struck Dorsey was over Sandy picked at her mind. If Sandy recognized Dorsey or her brother as the one who bashed in Arthur's head, would she keep that quiet? Velma said Butch and his sister were close. She'd seen the young man's rage. Of all the people at the lake that night, she could see him using an oar to kill someone. Why did Dorsey all of a sudden become so drunk? Was it remorse over killing Arthur and realizing he still wouldn't get the girl? Or remorse over lying about Coop? He *was* drinking a soda today.

Lost in thought, she recognized her turnoff too late. A glance in her rearview mirror said slamming on her brakes and turning was out of the question. A truck was driving too close to her back end. She sped up and watched for the next possible spot to get off the highway and turn around. A driveway gave her that chance.

She turned on her blinker and pulled into the drive. The truck roared on past.

"I was obviously going too slow for them." She swung her Jeep around and backtracked down the highway and onto the county road.

When she stopped at the T in the road to go right, she spotted a vehicle racing down the road behind her. Someone was in more of a hurry than she was. She turned right and continued, noting the other vehicle barely stopping at the T. Rolling her window down, she inhaled the pine scent heightened by the warm afternoon. The aroma reminded her of her house and studio tucked away on the mountain, embraced by large pine and fir trees. She missed her home. Missed Sheba and Lil.

A flash of black came into her peripheral vision moments before her Jeep lurched sideways.

She clutched the wheel and shoved her foot onto the brake, willing her vehicle to stay on four wheels as it careened sideways into the trees.

The Jeep slammed into a tree on the passenger side. The airbag in the steering wheel and driver's door slammed into her, taking her breath away, and emitting a foul smell. Her ribs and face hurt. White powder floated in the air making her blink. It took several minutes before she remembered she'd been forced off the road.

This time her muscles tensed from vigilance as she

unbuckled her seat belt. Ignoring the pain in her left side, she reached under her seat and grasped the handle of the pistol she carried in her Jeep for protection.

Ringing in her ears impeded her chances of hearing if anyone approached. She glanced out the front and side window. There wasn't a vehicle in sight. Had they expected to kill her? She hadn't been driving fast enough to cause her death. Was it a scare tactic? If so, she was more angry than scared.

She gripped the pistol, shoved her door open, and stepped out. Her legs wobbled, nearly folding. She leaned against the seat, scanning the interior of her vehicle for her purse. It was on the floor on the passenger side.

Her stomach heaved at the site of the Jeep door buckled inward. This was the first new vehicle she'd ever owned. The money from the sale of her first three vases had paid for it. Damn! Her sense of loss shifted to rage. Whoever did this was going to pay.

She crawled over the seat and reached down, hooking the shoulder strap of her purse. Back on her feet, she slung the strap over her shoulder and pulled her phone out of her bag. Her right hand still gripped the pistol.

Not knowing if her assailant had kept on going the same direction or turned around and headed back to the highway, she set out down the road toward the ranch. If anyone veered her direction, she'd shoot their tires.

She hit recent on her phone and found Logan's number.

"Officer Rider," he answered.

"Logan, it's Shandra. Someone ran me off the road—"

"Are you hurt? Where are you? You should have called nine-one-one."

"I'm shook up, not hurt. It's on Park City Loop Road about three miles from the ranch."

"You're breathing hard. What are you doing?"

She heard a siren in the background of the phone. "I'm walking to the ranch."

"No. Sit down and wait for me. But call the ranch and have someone come get you."

"I can—"

"If you don't call Jo, I will."

Swooshing sounds in her head made her sit down. "I'll call." She hit the red button and lay down. A wave of nausea rolled through her.

~*~

Ryan spotted Shandra's Jeep smashed against a tree. "Stop!" He flung the door open and hit the ground running. His chest tightened as he grasped the open door and found the vehicle empty.

"Over here!" shouted Andy.

He ran back to the road and discovered Andy, cradling Shandra's head on his lap. She was covered in the white powder from the air bags. The left side of her face was bruised. Her skin was so pale the bruising stood out. One hand lay open, her pistol sitting in the palm.

Had she shot at the person who ran her off the road? He picked up the pistol, tucked it into her purse, and slipped his hands underneath her.

"Shandra?" She didn't respond. He picked her up. "We need to get her to the doctor."

"The closest one is the agency." Andy jogged alongside of him as he carried her to the truck.

"We need to call this in."

A siren sounded in the distance.

"I think someone already has." Andy opened the driver's side door.

A tribal police vehicle slammed to a stop behind the truck. Officer Logan emerged from the SUV.

"How is she?" he asked, striding over.

"Unconscious. How did you know this happened?" Ryan narrowed his eyes at the man.

"She called. Told me she'd been run off the road and was going to walk to the ranch. I told her to call and have someone pick her up." His gaze drifted to the Jeep. He swore and shook his head.

"She was talking to you earlier. This could be on you." Ryan slid onto the truck seat, making sure he didn't bump Shandra into anything. "Let's get her to a doctor."

Rider closed the door. "I'll investigate here."

Shandra stirred in his arms. "No!" Her eyes opened. They fixed on him and slowly recognition dawned. "Ryan!" Her arms wrapped around his neck and she clung to him. That whisked away any suspicions he had that she cared about the officer.

He embraced her. "You're safe now. We're taking you to a doctor."

"No. Just take me to the ranch. I'm fine."

"We found you passed out. That's not fine."

"The detective is right. You should get checked out," Rider said through the down window.

"It was just shock. I'll be fine." She smiled at Andy. "Take me to the ranch."

He put the vehicle in gear and they started to pull away.

"I'll be there for your statement as soon as I get things squared away here." Rider backed away from the truck.

"What happened?" Ryan asked.

"Why would anyone want to crash me into trees?" Her golden eyes peered into his.

"Did you get a good look at them?"

"Not the person, only the truck. It was a big, black Chevy. It had followed close from Nespelem. When I missed the turnoff because I was running through things in my head, the truck went straight when I turned around. But they must have known where I was headed and turned the next chance they had and driven right up behind me again. I saw the truck catching up when I turned onto this road." She shuddered. "I was enjoying the pine trees and thinking of home when I caught a glimpse of the vehicle running beside me and the next minute I was slammed against the tree."

Ryan glanced over her head to Andy. Did he know who the truck belonged to? It appeared so. His knuckles were white he clutched the steering wheel so hard.

"Who did you and Velma talk to this morning?" he asked, pushing a stray strand of hair off her face.

"Dorsey, Lyle, and Billy. We talked about Arthur and drugs." Her eyes widened. "Do you think one of them, even though they swore to me they weren't involved, is?"

"How much did they tell you?"

"Enough that we went to Logan with all of it. He confirmed knowing some of it. They've been trying to catch the masterminds for six months." She leaned her head against his chest. "We have to find Arthur's killer soon. I want to go home."

He hugged her. He felt the same way. He wanted her safe and himself away from the suspicious eyes of Agent Weatherly.

~*~

Shandra woke up in the bed in Coop's room. Aunt Jo leaned over her.

"Good, you're awake. I was beginning to think these men should have ignored your request and took you to a doctor." Jo placed a hand on her forehead. "No temperature."

"There is no temperature with a concussion," Ryan said from somewhere behind Jo.

She turned her head and found him, sitting in the desk chair.

"How long have I been out?" She didn't like losing consciousness. It was safe in the ranch house but being unconscious made a person vulnerable.

"Twenty-thirty minutes." Ryan stood and walked over to the bed. "I need to ask Andy something, any chance you can stay awake while I'm gone?"

"What do you need to talk to him about?" She had a feeling he was keeping something from her. Something she needed to know.

"He didn't fill me in on what Weatherly had to say." He bent, kissing her forehead. "I'll be right back."

Her eyes narrowed as she watched him walk out the door.

"He's been sitting here the whole time waiting for you to wake up." Aunt Jo, nodded to her feet.

She wiggled her sock covered toes.

"He took off your boots and made you comfortable before I got up here." She smoothed her fingers over the wrinkles in Shandra's brow. "He's a good man. Don't let him go."

"But he keeps things from me." She mentally shook her head. He told me a secret no one else knew.

"He keeps things from you for your own good. Coop is home. They know Dorsey lied. There is no need for you to continue digging into this. He wants you safe and I want you safe." Aunt Jo jammed her fists onto her hips.

She looked so much like Velma, Shandra wanted to laugh but could tell by the fire in her eyes that would be a mistake.

"I'll tell Ryan to take you home tonight if you don't promise to quit asking questions that are putting you in danger."

"I promise, I won't be asking any more questions." She smiled at her aunt and knew she might not ask questions, but she had a whole heap of accusations for several people.

Coop stuck his head in the room. "Wow. I never thought you helping me would get you hurt."

"I'm fine. I didn't know helping you would get me

243

on the wrong side of drug dealers." She shrugged and her ribs twinged. "Oh!"

"You okay?" Coop stepped into the room and his mother sat down on the bed next to her.

"What's wrong?" Jo asked.

"I think the side air bag bruised my ribs." She rubbed a hand over her left side. "Where's Sandy?"

"Ruby came by and picked her up. She wanted to get some information from her house. Stuff she needs for school." Coop leaned against the door jamb.

Shandra sat up. "It's not safe for her to be running around. Rumors have spread about her witnessing the murder."

"She'll be fine. I called Lyle. He's going to be tailing her. You know, to keep her safe." Coop shoved away from the door jamb.

"Why didn't you take her?" It would have made more sense for Coop to escort his girl than leave it up to his friend.

He nodded toward his mother. "She thinks I'll be assassinated if I leave the ranch."

Aunt Jo's face deepened in color.

Shandra laughed, ignoring her sore ribs.

"It's good to hear you laughing." Logan eased Coop out of the doorway and entered.

The room was getting smaller and smaller by the minute with so many bodies crowding in.

"I don't suppose my Jeep will be drivable." She didn't want to think about having to find a new one. She loved her copper Jeep.

"I've seen worse accidents where the vehicle drove

off, but you're going to want that frame looked at. It could have tweaked or bent from the impact." He sat in the desk chair. It squeaked and disappeared.

Aunt Jo waved her hands like she was shooing chickens. "Come on Coop, this is official business, we need to leave Logan to his questions."

Coop rolled his eyes but left the room, followed by his mother.

Logan grinned and shook his head. "That Jo is something else. Wish she'd had a daughter. I might be tempted to marry then."

Shandra smiled. She could see Logan married to a woman like Aunt Jo.

"Who's getting married?" Ryan asked, entering the room and sitting on the bed next to her.

He picked up her hand, lacing their fingers. Her heart expanded at the knowledge he loved her and trusted her.

"Logan said if Aunt Jo had a daughter he'd marry her." She noted when she said it, the big man's face deepened to a crimson color.

"You have any cousins like your aunt?" Ryan asked.

She laughed and Logan cleared his throat.

"I'm here to fill out Shandra's statement about the accident."

She repeated everything that happened. "I wish I had a good look at the driver, but my gaze went to the side of the vehicle as it crashed into my Jeep. And when the truck was behind me, I just noticed the color and make, not the driver."

Ryan shifted. Her gaze latched onto his face as he nodded toward the door.

Logan stood and headed for the door.

"I'll walk Logan out and be right back," he said.

"You know who the truck belongs to." She stared into his eyes, daring him to lie to her.

He stared back and sighed. "Rider, come back in the room."

That's what he was keeping from her. Why he had to talk to Andy. Her cousin must have recognized the truck from her description.

Logan stepped back into the room. His gaze jumped back and forth between them.

"From Shandra's description, Andy believes the truck belongs to Butch Williams, Sandy's brother." Ryan focused on her. "You said you'd been asking about the drugs coming onto the reservation. Either someone overheard or one of the three you talked to said something to Butch."

She shook her head. "None of them acted like they cared much for him or the drugs coming to the reservation." It didn't make sense. She didn't believe any of those three had anything to do with Arthur's death, and she didn't think they would help Butch or the drug dealers.

Chapter Twenty-nine

Shandra couldn't believe the attention she received from not only Ryan but the rest of the family. Saturday morning, Aunt Jo made her favorite waffles for breakfast. Before the meal was finished, Velma arrived with a jar of huckleberry jam and insisted she have another half a waffle with the jam.

Andy and Coop offered to tow her Jeep to Omak for her insurance to do an appraisal. Even Uncle Martin suggested if she felt up to it, she and Ryan should take a horseback ride.

The only person who didn't smother her was Sandy. She'd returned with Ruby the night before sometime after dark, carrying a cardboard filing box. This morning she was in the bedroom, digging out the information she needed for a scholarship. That's what Coop said when Shandra asked him about Sandy.

"We going to talk to anybody today?" Velma

asked, helping herself to a waffle and a good portion of the jam she'd brought.

"She isn't talking to anyone other than family today," Ryan said, raising a cup of coffee to his lips.

She glared at him. "You know how I feel about other people making decisions for me."

"It's only because I care about you. Tomorrow, I'm taking you home."

That only made her dig her heels in more. "I'm not going back until the killer is found."

"That could take months. I know for a fact you have a show coming up in August and nothing new to show there. I'd think you need to get back to your studio and get to work."

He had her there. She did need to get to work. But family came first.

Ryan's phone beeped. He glanced at the screen and headed for the door.

With him out of earshot, she faced Velma. "Someone we talked to yesterday had to have tipped off Butch. Which one do you think was lying to us?"

Her cousin chewed on the bite of waffle in her mouth and then said, "I would have bet my huckleberry jam recipe that none of them lied."

"Then how did Butch find out we talked to the police about the drugs?" She picked up her tea cup and sipped. When she'd awaken this morning she'd been disappointed Ella hadn't come to her in a dream. She was missing something and needed guidance.

Jo walked out of the kitchen, leaving her and Velma alone. Leaning close, she asked, "Is there a way to invite Ella into my dreams?"

Velma's smile widened, spreading across her face nearly from one ear to the other. Her eyes lit up. "You believe in the dreams."

"I believe that Grandmother has helped me solve puzzling murders. She didn't come to me last night and I feel like I'm missing something."

"She'll come to you tonight." Velma nodded.

"How do you know that? Did you talk to her?"

"No. Because you now truly believe." Velma stood. "Why don't you go enjoy some time with that policeman of yours. As long as you stay on the ranch, you'll be safe."

Shandra stared at the closed door after Velma left. She did believe in the dreams and her grandmother. The notion settled easily in her heart and her mind.

Ryan returned. The scowl on his face tossed all her thoughts away.

"What's wrong?"

"Andy and I found an oar floating on the edge of the lake yesterday. There was some hair in the cracks of the wooden paddle. He showed the police, and they sent it off for testing. The hair wasn't the victim's and there wasn't any trace of blood on it. They found over fifty different prints." He poured another cup of coffee. "I was sure that was the murder weapon." He sat down across the table from her.

"That would have been too easy." She half-smiled at him.

"I guess so. We probably won't find the murder weapon until we find the murderer." He sipped his coffee and watched her over the brim. "How are you feeling this morning?"

"A little sore, not bad. How do I look?" She'd cringed at the sight of her purple face in the mirror earlier.

"Like a woman who was in a car wreck." He tipped his head toward the door. "Feel up to a horseback ride before it gets too hot?"

"I'd love one."

As if on cue, Aunt Jo returned with a small backpack and started filling two water bottles with ice and water, and bagging cookies.

"Were you listening in?" Shandra accused her aunt.

"No. You both looked interested when Martin suggested a ride. I went in search of Andy's old school backpack."

"Did you disturb Sandy, searching Andy's room?" She'd never seen Sandy upset about anything. Frightened and meek but not angry upset.

"No. She wasn't in the room. There was music in the bathroom. I think she was getting ready for a shower."

Ryan took the pack from Aunt Jo, and they headed out to find Uncle Martin had two horses saddled and waiting for them.

She hugged her uncle. "Thank you. This is exactly what I needed."

"Nothing better than getting outdoors to get closer to the Creator." He held the reins of her horse while she stepped into the stirrup and swung into the saddle.

"I agree. I hope we get this cleared up soon so I can

get back to my mountain." She patted the horse on the neck. It was an appaloosa. The only breed raised on the Higheagle Ranch. The horse of their ancestors.

She looked over her shoulder and the spotted rump of her mount, at Ryan. He sat atop a sorrel horse with a white blanketed rump covered in black spots of varying sizes. "Ready?"

"Yep."

They headed out of the barnyard toward the area where Andy took her to see Coop when she'd arrived here nearly a week ago.

~*~

Sitting under the tree where she'd talked to Coop, Shandra sipped her water and nibbled on a cookie as Ryan read an email on his phone.

He glanced up. "The forensics are back on the body. The coroner believes he was hit alongside the head with a limb. They found fragments of willow bark embedded in his skull."

"She lied." The distraught face of Sandy came to her mind. The way the young woman avoided physical contact with Coop. Was it because she loved someone else or because she knew how he would feel knowing she killed someone?

"Who lied? Sandy?"

"Yes. Why would she say someone hit him with an oar? She made up the story to cover for the fact she killed him." She chewed on her bottom lip. "But why allow Coop to go to jail for the crime? Especially, if she loved him."

Ryan slid over beside her. "She doesn't love him."

251

She gazed into Ryan's eyes and witnessed what she didn't see between Sandy and Coop.

"Why does Coop dote on her when he doesn't love her? Because you're right. I've been trying to figure out their feelings for one another and she doesn't love him. But the way he talks about her, I thought he loved her." She was confused. Not confused about the man sitting next to her but relationships in general.

"Go back to yesterday," Ryan said, picking a cookie out of a bag. "When you were talking to those three at the bar, who seemed most interested in Sandy?"

"Dorsey. He admitted to liking her the first time I talked to him, and he fingered Coop hoping to get Sandy. I would bet Sandy didn't kill Arthur. I don't see it in her, but Dorsey…He'd built up a lot of anger toward Arthur." She thought about his drunken state. She'd wondered if it was remorse over killing his friend. That was the way it looked right now.

"He could have called Sandy, told her what was talked about. She could have called her brother. You said they were close. And he decided to do a little scaring of his own." Ryan put an arm around her shoulders and drew her near, placing a kiss on her head. "I'm glad all he did was try to scare you."

"Me too. But instead of scaring me it made me more determined to discover who did kill Arthur and why."

Ryan stood and held out his hand to help her to her feet. "She's covering for one of two people. Dorsey or Butch."

Shandra stood. "I think we need to visit with her

when we get back to the house."

"I agree."

~*~

Ryan scanned the area as they rode up to the ranch house and barn. Coop's pickup was missing and Agent Weatherly's SUV sat behind his truck.

There was no way he could send Shandra in to say he'd taken off again. The agent would know he was avoiding him and that would make him even more suspicious. The best thing to do was act normal.

At the barn, he dismounted and held Shandra's horse while she dismounted. He leaned toward her for a kiss. "Weatherly's here. Go on in. I can't avoid him forever. I'll put the horses up."

She kissed him and walked to the house.

He could count on her keeping the agent busy with questions.

What bothered him more at the moment was Coop leaving the ranch when this was the only safe place for him until they found the real killer. Granted he'd have to go to school when it started, but he'd be off the reservation and away from the vengeful Randal family.

One horse was unsaddled when Martin wandered into the barn. "Thought I'd come help. Seemed like you were taking a long time."

He shook his head. "Thinking more than unsaddling. Shandra won't go home until this is solved. So it needs to be solved to keep her safe and get her home."

Her uncle moved him aside and finished unsaddling the horse Ryan had ridden. "Our police and the FBI will figure it out. Maybe I should say something to Shandra, give her permission to leave."

"Why would she need permission?" There were times he didn't understand things her family said. Like now. He spoke a language Ryan knew but it didn't make sense.

The man faced him, his brown eyes studied him, and his mouth formed a firm line. "She has been away from the family. Now that she is back, she feels she must do more than others to help. Her guilt over not being with her grandmother all these years compels her to try and do right by all. If I, or Jo, give her permission to let this go, she will abide by her elders. She is learning the truth about family."

What her uncle said made sense. But he didn't know Shandra. His experience with the stubborn woman told him she would not leave until the murderer was found.

Before he could bring that to the man's attention, the sound of someone approaching stopped the conversation. He pivoted and found Agent Weatherly walking toward them.

"Detective Greer, I'd begun to think you were avoiding me." The man's gaze bore into him.

"No. I didn't know you were looking for me. I've been busy."

"Yes, sending the police on bogus evidence retrievals." Weatherly glanced over at Martin. "I'm sure you have other things to do."

Martin glanced at him.

"Go ahead. Agent Weatherly can help me put the

horses out." He didn't hide the grin spreading across his face at the tortured expression on the agent's face.

Martin also grinned and walked out of the barn.

"Here you go. Just walk and the horse will follow." He handed the lead rope to the horse he'd ridden to Weatherly.

The agent grasped the rope in his hand with a death grip.

His actions only added to the delight Ryan received from watching the man handle the horse.

At the corral, he opened the gate and walked in with the other dozen horses milling about. He released the horse and turned to the gate. Weatherly stood outside the gate, his face pale.

"Come on in. They aren't going to get you." He waved the agent to walk into the corral.

Agent Weatherly held the rope out to him. "Here. You're in there already."

He walked over, gathered the lead rope, opened the gate, and led the horse in. He released the horse and slipped out the gate. "Not a horse person?" he asked, walking into the barn.

"No. You seem at home with them." The man fell into step beside him.

"Grew up on a sheep ranch in Idaho. Horses were a step up from riding sheep." He expected a laugh. After hanging the lead rope, he faced the agent and found the man contemplating something.

"You rode sheep?" the man asked, his voice low and uncertain.

Ryan laughed so hard his belly hurt. The agent's

face grew redder by the minute as he continued to laugh.

He gathered himself and said, "As kids we rode sheep for fun, but people don't really ride them. You're not a farm boy are you?"

"I grew up in the city only seeing animals at the zoo." Weatherly stopped before they started out the door of the barn. "You look familiar but I can't place it. You sure you don't remember doing anything with the FBI?"

He shook his head. "I don't remember doing anything with the FBI." In good conscience, he hadn't learned of the FBI's involvement in the gang fiasco until after the fact.

"Why did you think that oar was the murder weapon?"

He liked the man could switch to business in a blink of an eye. "Sandy said she saw the man in the boat hit the victim with an oar. I spotted the oar, saw it had hair in the cracks and suspected it was the weapon."

"You can quit looking for an oar. Forensics came back that it was a willow limb. Lots of those along that lake." Weatherly studied him. "But you'd know that since you seemed to have hiked around it yesterday."

"If it was a willow limb, why did Sandy say it was an oar?" He could deflect comments, too.

"That's what I came to ask her, but it seems she took off with Coop Elwood's truck an hour before I arrived."

"Did you ask Coop where she went?" The second

he said it he remembered the two brothers were towing Shandra's Jeep. "Never mind. He's not here."

"I thought he was staying at the ranch." The agent narrowed his eyes.

"He and Andy are towing Shandra's Jeep to Omak." He narrowed his eyes on the agent. "She was forced off the road yesterday. The collision with a tree did extensive damage to her Jeep."

"I'd heard there had been an accident. I didn't realize until I saw her face that it had been Miss Higheagle."

"You'd think you and the tribal police would keep each other better informed." Which gave him an idea. "I discovered a house yesterday on my walk that I wouldn't be surprised was part of the drug movement in this reservation. I'm telling you because every time the police get a tip and go for a raid the place is cleaned out."

"Someone on the force is tipping them off." The agent caught on quick.

"Yes. But if the raid were to come from the feds and no one in the tribal police knew about it…"

"We could catch them. Come on. Show me this place on the map." The agent led the way to his SUV. He opened the back and pulled out a laptop computer. He opened it and brought Google Maps up. Buffalo Lake took up the full screen.

He spotted the area where the party was held and the dock and traced his finger along the shoreline to the residence. "There. Two men in fancy clothes drove up in a new car. They went in this small construction trailer. There were three voices, but the drone of the fan kept me from hearing what they were talking about."

Agent Weatherly's lips tipped into a calculating smile. "We'll get surveillance on them and pick the best time for a raid. Thanks for the tip." He shut the laptop and pulled out his phone.

"Any time." He walked away from the SUV and to the house. With the agent focused on taking down the drug traffickers, Ryan hoped he forgot about recognizing him.

Chapter Thirty

"What do you mean she drove off in Coop's truck?" Shandra stood in the kitchen, staring at her aunt.

"She said Butch called and she needed to go home to help with their mother." Jo held a spatula in the air and her other hand was on her hip. "I won't get between a child and her mother."

She wasn't worried someone would harm the young woman. It was clear she wasn't in any danger. But she was running.

"What is wrong with her mother?" If it was a medical or emotional crisis, she could see where Sandy would be of more use than her callous brother.

"She's been unstable since her husband died. I heard she drinks herself into pity parties and then tries to kill herself." Jo shook her head. "It's a shame the things some parents put their children through. That's why Coop has been there for Sandy. He knew about her unstable home life and how hard she worked to get money to go to college. She wants off the reservation and away from the melodrama of her mother."

She understood the goal to get away from parents. She'd lived that life, too.

Ryan came through the door. Talking with Aunt Jo she'd forgotten Agent Weatherly had gone to the barn looking for him.

"How'd it go?" She crossed the room to be strong for him.

"Good. He's rounding up agents to do a raid on that house I discovered yesterday." He rubbed a hand up and down her arm.

She studied his face but didn't learn anything. Asking him if the man figured out where he knew him from in front of her aunt was out of the question.

"Why did Sandy take Coop's truck?" he asked.

"To help her brother with her mother." Even as she said it, her gut clenched. Something else was up.

Ryan must have felt the same. "Let's go help them out."

She kissed his cheek. "I was thinking the same thing. I'll go get my purse." She raced up the stairs and grabbed her purse. The door to Andy's room was open. The contents of the filing box were scattered over the bed. She crossed to the bed and scanned the papers. They were ledgers of shipments of drugs. In the middle of the bed sat a pink check book. She picked it up. Deposits for five thousand dollars were circled. A glance at the papers on the bed, she noticed dates circled on the pages.

Ryan appeared at her side. "What's taking so long?"

She showed him the check book and one of the pages. "I think Sandy figured out her schooling was being funded by her brother's drug money."

"How did she get the ledger pages?" He picked them up and dumped them in the filing box. "This is what she came back with last night. Where did she find it?"

"I don't know, but I think we better find her before she gets herself killed." Shandra dropped the check book on top of the papers and put the lid on the box. "Is Weatherly still here?"

"He left five minutes ago." Ryan picked up the box and headed for the stairs.

Shandra followed, scrolled through her recent calls and pushed on a number.

"Hey, Shandra. Are you feeling better today?" Logan's caring voice made her smile.

"Yes, I'm fine. We need to find Butch and Sandy Williams. We think Sandy may be in danger from her brother. Ryan and I are at the ranch and headed to Nespelem. We have evidence that your chief might find interesting." She hurried out of the house behind Ryan. He held the passenger door open for her on his truck.

"Why do you think Butch will hurt his sister?"

"Because she just found out his drug dealing has been funding her college." She slid in the truck as Ryan put the box of evidence in the bench seat behind and started the engine.

"Call me if you find them." She hung up as Ryan shot down the driveway.

"If she didn't know about Butch until now, why did she lie about seeing someone hit Arthur with an oar?" Shandra's head swirled with all the information she'd gathered the past week.

"Sandy could have killed Arthur." Ryan glanced over at her.

"You've seen her. Do you really think she's strong enough to swing a limb and hit hard enough to kill a person?" That was the part she had trouble with. Seeing the meek young woman come up with the strength both mentally and physically to kill someone.

"It's amazing the strength people find when pushed to their limit."

"But why kill him? Because he attacked her? I don't see her going back to avenge her attacker. Besides Coop came to her rescue and did a number on the guy." She studied Ryan's profile. "If you beat someone up who'd harmed me, I'd find that chivalrous and not go after the guy myself. You could do far more damage than I could."

He placed a hand on her leg. "You know I'd protect you with my life if need be."

"I don't want that to ever happen." She put her hand over his, and they rode like that the rest of the way to Nespelem.

At Sandy's house, Coop's truck sat in the driveway. She didn't see Butch's black truck that everyone believed tried to run her off the road.

"We can't go in without a warrant," Ryan said,

walking over to Coop's truck and looking inside.

"We can knock on the door." She marched up to the door and knocked. Silence.

"I don't think they're here." Ryan joined her on the stoop.

"But how will we figure out where they could be?" She moved to the front window and peered in. "The mother should be here."

She pulled out her phone and called Velma.

"Hello."

"It's Shandra. Could you call Sandy's mom for me and ask her where Butch is?"

"Why would you want to know that?" The woman used her drill sergeant tone.

"I'm standing outside the house and knocking and no one is answering. Sandy may be in danger." She squinted, trying to see inside the dark house.

"Ok. I'll call. This time of day she should be puttering around the house."

Shandra disconnected and waited. The house phone rang and rang. No one answered. She expected Velma to call her right back. When ten minutes had passed, she called her cousin and got a busy signal.

"We need to look for them," Ryan said.

"We need to get in the house and see if there's a clue to where they could be. And where is the mother?"

A wide-bodied car came around the corner and stopped behind Coop's truck. Velma and Ruby's mother emerged from the vehicle.

"I brought Helen along to open the door. She has a key." Velma stopped at the edge of the stoop.

Shandra hugged Velma. "That was a good idea." She stepped back so Mrs. Perkins could unlock the door.

"I've had this key for years and this is the first time I've had to use it," Mrs. Perkins said, shoving the key in and turning the knob. The door opened and the house smelled like a skunk had been let loose.

"What is that awful smell," Velma asked, putting an arm in front of her nose.

"Marijuana. Butch must have been having a party while his sister was away." Ryan opened the windows.

Shandra flipped the light switch. The house looked like a bachelor pad. Clothes, beer cans and food wrappers were strewn about.

"I can't believe Alice would put up with this." Mrs. Perkins wandered down the hall. "Alice! Alice, where are you?"

Shandra moved about reading every piece of paper she spied.

"On no!" Mrs. Perkins exclamation sent everyone rushing down the hall. They found her in the middle of a room with a stripped bed.

"What's wrong?" Velma asked, moving to put an arm around the distraught woman's shoulders.

"This is Alice's room. Look in the closet. There aren't any clothes. There isn't anything of Alice left in here." Her eyes glistened with tears. "Where is she?"

"When was the last time you saw her?" Ryan asked.

"A month or two ago. She stayed at home, to herself." Mrs. Perkins didn't meet anyone's gaze.

"Because she drank and didn't want people to see her drunk?" Shandra asked softly.

"Yes. After losing her husband she fell into the bottle."

Velma rolled her eyes.

"When was the last time you talked to her? Surely, when Sandy arrived at your house after the attack." She studied the woman. Her features crumbled.

"I tried to call over here, but no one answered. I figured she was drinking and Sandy was better off at our house." Her mouth dropped open and then snapped shut. "Do you think she was gone then?"

"It's possible." Ryan opened and closed the empty dresser drawers using a rubber glove he must have had in his pocket.

"Hello? Anyone here?" Logan's voiced boomed through the room.

"Back here," Ryan called.

Shandra didn't like the feeling she was getting about the two missing siblings.

Logan ducked his head and stepped into the small room, pushing Shandra up against Ryan and Velma and Mrs. Perkins to sit on the bed.

"What's going on?" he pulled out a notepad.

Ryan put his arm around her and said, "It appears Mrs. Williams is missing as well as her children."

The officer nodded to Mrs. Perkins and Velma. "When did you notice Mrs. Williams was missing?"

Mrs. Perkins burst into tears.

"Right now," Velma said.

"Oh!" He took a step forward and patted Mrs.

Perkins shoulder. "I'm sorry. Can I get a statement?"

"Come on," Ryan clasped her hand, leading her from the room. "He doesn't need us, but we need to find Sandy and Butch." They walked out of the house and climbed into his truck.

"Where do we look?" she asked.

"We're pretty sure this had to do with drugs. I think we should go to either the house I found or Rebecca Lake, the drop off point for shipments."

"I vote for the lake. It would be a good place to get rid of a body. Either their mother's or Sandy's if she confronted Butch."

Chapter Thirty-one

Ryan took the highway bypassing the agency to the Buffalo Lake Road which wound by Rebecca Lake. This route allowed him to drive faster. From the way Shandra played with the fringe on her purse, he could tell she was as anxious as he was about getting to the lake in time to save a life. Whose, he wasn't sure.

A less used dirt road took off through the sage brush on the curve before he spotted the main entrance. His gut told him to take the dirt road, but his mind had other ideas. He continued to the main entrance to the lake.

A dirt parking area and boat launch area with an outhouse was empty.

"The road continues," Shandra pointed to a road on the opposite side of the parking area.

He steered the truck to that road and continued slowly to not raise too much dust. The road connected with the first road he'd wanted to take. The dirt track went alongside what appeared to be a slough.

"There's the truck that ran me off the road." Her finger pointed at a black truck twenty-five yards off the road.

He slipped in behind the truck. "Call Rider and tell him where we are and that we've found Butch's truck. I'm going to get closer and see what's going on."

She put a hand on his arm. "Be careful."

He leaned over, opened the glove box, and took out his Glock and handcuffs. Before straightening, he placed a kiss on her lips. "I will."

The sagebrush was fairly tall, gathering moisture from the lake. He crouched behind the bushes, making his way to the edge of the slough. A shout stopped his forward movement.

"I said dig!" The male voice had a high, almost hysterical pitch.

He couldn't hear the reply, only the low pitch which told him the other person was also a male. Ryan glanced back at the truck. Shandra was on her cell phone. They were expecting to find Sandy and Butch. A female and male.

Inching closer, he slipped behind another bush, and yet another, until he could see the two people. One held a shotgun. The other was digging in the soft mud at the edge of the slough. He didn't have a clue who either of the young men were. Shandra had kept him at the ranch where he'd had limited access to the people of interest.

"This is stupid, Dorsey," the one digging said. "I don't care if you killed Arthur. Shit, you can use my dealing drugs to keep me quiet about that."

"Shut up! The only reason people care about Arthur's death is because Coop's nosey cousin showed up and started digging and proving he didn't do it." He waved the shotgun. "Get on with it. I know this is where you buried your mother. Once I show Sandy what you did, she'll be grateful to me. You'll be out of the way, and I'll take care of her."

Hearing Sandy wasn't around relieved Ryan. It was just the two young men he had to deal with. From the conversation, he figured the one digging was Butch, Sandy's brother. But if Sandy wasn't here, where was she?

He had to keep Dorsey from shooting Butch until reinforcements arrived. The way Dorsey held the shotgun, he knew how to use it. He was far enough away from Butch, the other young man couldn't strike out at him with the shovel.

The best scenario was to sneak up behind Dorsey and wrestle the shotgun from him and hope Butch didn't get to his pickup before he subdued Dorsey.

He shoved his Glock into his waistband at his lower back and eased his way to the bushes directly behind the young man holding the shotgun.

~*~

Shandra tossed her phone into her bag and stepped out of the truck. Logan was sending help. But until then she needed to make sure no one left the area. Ryan had left the keys in the ignition. She pulled those, slipping them into her pocket.

The black truck didn't have a key in the ignition.

269

That meant whoever drove it here had the key. She pulled the hood latch inside and went to the front of the vehicle and found the hook, releasing the hood the rest of the way. A grin twitched her lips. She mentally thanked Orville, the ranch foreman on her stepfather's ranch, for making sure she could take care of any mechanical problems with her vehicle. She pulled the coil wire to the distributor cap and tossed it into the bushes. Careful to not make a sound, she lowered the hood. No one was going to leave here before reinforcements came.

What was Ryan doing? Only way she knew to find out was to find him. Taking care to stay low behind the bushes, she made her way toward the smelly inlet of the lake. The voice she heard talking stalled her feet. What was Dorsey doing here? Moving closer, she spotted the shotgun in his hands.

Her mind clicked back over all her conversations with him. She'd found him volatile and insolent the first time she'd talked with him. The second time he'd been drunk. And the third…quiet and retrospective. But each time the one thing that had remained true was his affection for Sandy.

Where was she? He wouldn't hold a gun to her. Would he?

She crept forward through the sagebrush and caught a glimpse of the person he held at gunpoint. Butch.

This didn't make sense. The whole murder from the beginning hadn't made sense.

A flicker of color in her peripheral vision drew her

attention. Ryan was sneaking up behind Dorsey. She held her breath as he leaped and caught the young man around the waist.

Boom! The shotgun blasted, but missed Butch. He didn't waste any time running for the vehicle.

She ran to where Ryan and Dorsey rolled on the ground.

"Stop!" Ryan wrenched the young man's arms behind him, locking the handcuffs around his wrists. He pulled Dorsey to his feet and picked up the shotgun. "Where did the other one go?"

"He ran to the trucks." Shandra studied Dorsey. He was wild-eyed and agitated.

"We need to stop him." Ryan shoved Dorsey in front of him toward the trucks.

"He can only get away on foot." Shandra patted her pocket.

A grin spread across Ryan's face. "You have the keys to both trucks?"

"No, only ours. I didn't find any in the other one, so I pulled the coil wire."

"I could kiss you."

Sirens whined, growing closer.

"Here, hold him, while I catch Butch." Ryan released Dorsey and ran toward the vehicles.

Shandra linked her arm through the young man's, leading him the direction Ryan disappeared. "I don't understand, Dorsey. Why were you making Butch dig at gun point?"

"He buried his mother there. I wanted him to dig up the body. Then I could show Sandy she couldn't count on her brother. She'd have to turn to me."

She couldn't believe the young man's irrational thinking. "Where is Sandy? She took Coop's truck to meet Butch. The truck is at the house."

He stopped and stared at her. "Butch said he took the truck to teach Coop a lesson."

"What lesson? Why would Butch want to teach Coop a lesson?" She was getting more and more confused as she talked to Dorsey.

The wailing of the sirens ended. Shouts and car doors slamming invaded the sounds of nature.

She pulled Dorsey out of the bushes. Three tribal police vehicles still had lights flashing, but not a soul was in sight.

"None of what you're saying is making any sense. Do you know who killed Arthur?"

A smile twisted his lips. "I did. He'd gone too far attacking Sandy and then telling me she would never love me. She didn't want to associate with the bastard of a drunk." His laugh stood the hair on her arms. "I showed him I had balls. He was always telling me I didn't have the balls to do this or to do that. Things that would ruin my chances of getting out of here. I had balls to keep my nose clean and dream of a day when I'd be working on the outside and not have to smell the stench of my father's house."

The thud of running feet caught her attention. She shoved Dorsey into the back of a police vehicle and crouched by the door. If it was Butch she wasn't going to become his bargaining chip.

"Shandra!" Ryan's voice boomed.

She stood. "Over here."

Sweat glistened on his forehead. He grasped her arms and pulled her into a hug. "We lost him, but the feds have a helicopter in the area. They're searching now." His gaze drifted to the back of the police vehicle. "He killed Arthur Randal."

"I know. He told me. But I'm worried about Sandy. Where is she?" Shandra looked skyward as the thump, thump, thump of helicopter blades cutting the air, grew in volume.

"Dorsey said Butch said he took Coop's truck. That doesn't make sense. Why would he cover for Sandy? Unless he killed his sister like he did his mother." A shiver slithered down her spine.

"I'm taking you to the ranch. Tomorrow we're going home. You've proved Coop didn't commit murder and found the person who did."

She wasn't going to argue with him. Seeing the state Dorsey was in, she didn't care to hang around.

A Tribal officer arrived as they walked to the truck.

"There's a murder suspect in that car," Ryan said, pointing to the vehicle.

The officer saluted and stood by the vehicle.

"Come on. They can get our statements at the ranch."

Chapter Thirty-two

Shandra finished her shower and walked into Coop's bedroom, drying her hair. The dogs started barking. She went to the window and watched Agent Weatherly's SUV drive up behind Ryan's truck.

Great. Just what they didn't need. After dinner, she and Ryan had spent over an hour repeating their actions of the afternoon to the tribal police. Now the agent was here to badger them. She pulled a robe on around her skimpy, summer, baby doll pajamas and headed down to the kitchen.

To her surprise Sandy was with Agent Weatherly.

"Sandy, we've been worried about you." Aunt Jo crossed the room and hugged the young woman.

Tears slipped down Sandy's cheeks as she hugged Jo. Her gaze landed on Coop, sitting at the table. She pushed out of Jo's arms and knelt by Coop. "I'm sorry for all the lies. I didn't know what to do. When I started to suspect Butch was bringing in the drugs, I went to Chief George, he connected me with Agent Weatherly. I've been working with him to help stop the drugs coming onto the reservation. But it wasn't enough to stop my mother from overdosing."

Coop brushed a tear off her cheek. "I knew something was up when you called and said you only wanted to be friends."

"Miss Williams has been gathering evidence for us. When this Randal attacked her at the lake, we thought it was because Butch had told him his sister was asking too many questions. When he ended up dead, we didn't know what to think." Agent Weatherly accepted a cup of coffee from Aunt Jo.

"But why have Sandy lie?" Shandra didn't like lies no matter who they saved from pain.

"Because she wasn't near the lake. After Coop dropped her off, she found more evidence against her brother and discovered her mother's death. She called me. I picked her up, took her to her aunt's in Omak, and then had agents keep an eye on the house."

"Why keep her mother's death quiet?" Ryan walked up behind Shandra, slipping an arm around her middle.

"We wanted to see what Butch did. She had to have gotten into the drugs he was to sell. He took the body out during the night. He called Dorsey to help him."

"That's why he was drunk the next time Velma and I talked to him. He was feeling guilty for not telling Sandy about her mother. But he wasn't guilty about

275

killing Arthur." A chill chased through her at the memory of Dorsey's unstable mind. She pushed closer to Ryan for warmth and comfort.

"Did you get the guys at the house by the lake?" Ryan asked.

Agent Weatherly smiled. "We did. By not going through the tribal police, they didn't have the place cleaned out. I think we might have taken care of the drug problem for now. But it will be right back. When there are so many wanting it, they find a way to get it."

Coop stood, pulling Sandy to her feet. "Let's go for a walk."

This time Shandra saw the spark in both their eyes that she'd been missing. She glanced up at Ryan. He saw it too.

All was right for her family again. She was ready to go home.

About the Author

Thank you for returning to the Colville Reservation with Shandra. I've been honored to call an author who lives on the Colville Reservation a friend. She is my go-to person to make sure my depiction of the reservation is accurate and I don't offend anyone. I'm excited for you to read the next book in the series, *Yuletide Slayings*. This will be available November 2016. As the title predicts, it is set during Christmas time and is full of suspense and mystery.

If you enjoyed this book, please leave a review. It is the best way to repay an author for your hours of entertainment and their months of writing the book.

I love to hear from fans. You can contact me through my website, blog, or newsletter. By joining my newsletter you get access to my books for free. Join and find out how. You can also find me on Goodreads, Facebook, and Pinterest.

All my work has Western or Native American elements in them along with hints of humor and engaging characters. My husband and I raise alfalfa hay in rural eastern Oregon. Riding horses and battling rattlesnakes, I not only write the western lifestyle, I live it.

patyjager.net

patyjager.blogspot.com

Windtree
Press

Thank you for purchasing this Windtree Press
publication. For other books of the heart, please visit
our website at www.windtreepress.com.

For questions or more information contact us
at info@windtreepress.com.

Windtree Press
www.windtreepress.com
Hillsboro, OR 97124

Made in the USA
Las Vegas, NV
19 May 2022